SMALL
STEPS

OTHER BOOKS BY LOUIS SACHAR

Holes

Stanley Yelnats' Survival Guide to Camp Green Lake

Dogs Don't Tell Jokes

The Boy Who Lost His Face

There's a Boy in the Girls' Bathroom

Awards for
HOLES

Winner of the Newbery Medal

Winner of the National Book Award

Winner of the *Boston Globe–Horn Book* Award

An ALA Best Book for Young Adults

An ALA Notable Book

An ALA Quick Pick

Winner of the Christopher Award for Juvenile Fiction

A *New York Times Book Review* Notable Children's
Book of the Year

A *Horn Book* Fanfare

A *Publishers Weekly* Best Book of the Year

A *Bulletin* Blue Ribbon Book

A *School Library Journal* Best Book of the Year

Praise for
HOLES

"A smart jigsaw puzzle of a novel."—*The New York Times Book Review*

"[A] rugged, engrossing adventure."   —*School Library Journal*

"Larger-than-life."   —*Publishers Weekly*

LOUIS SACHAR

SMALL STEPS

DELACORTE PRESS

Published by Delacorte Press
an imprint of Random House Children's Books
a division of Random House, Inc.
New York

Delacorte Press and colophon are registered trademarks of Random House, Inc.

www.randomhouse.com/kids

Educators and librarians, for a variety of teaching tools, visit us at
www.randomhouse.com/teachers

The Library of Congress has cataloged the hardcover edition of this work as follows:

Sachar, Louis.
Small Steps / Louis Sachar.
p. cm.
Summary: Three years after being released from Camp Green Lake, Armpit is trying
hard to keep his life on track.
ISBN 978-0-385-73314-4 (trade) — ISBN 978-0-385-90333-2 (Gibraltar lib. bdg.)
[1. Juvenile delinquents—Rehabilitation—Fiction. 2. Cerebral palsy—Fiction.
3. People with disabilities—Fiction. 4. Singers—Fiction. 5. Interpersonal relations—
Fiction. 6. African Americans—Fiction.] I. Title.
PZ7.S1185Sma 2006
[Fic]—dc22
2005009102

ISBN: 978-0-385-73315-1 (trade pbk.)
Printed in the United States of America

10 9 8 7 6 5 4 3

First Trade Paperback Edition

To Laura and Nancy,
for all you taught me

SMALL
STEPS

1

Once again Armpit was holding a shovel, only now he was getting paid for it, seven dollars and sixty-five cents an hour. He worked for Raincreek Irrigation and Landscaping. He was in the process of digging a trench along the side yard of a house that belonged to the mayor of Austin, a woman with the unusual name of Cherry Lane. As his shovel knifed through the dirt, he carefully kept the sod intact so that it could be replaced later. His shovel was short and had a rectangular blade, unlike the five-foot shovels with pointed blades he had used when he was at Camp Green Lake Juvenile Correctional Facility.

Beads of perspiration rolled out from under his red RAINCREEK cap. His shirt was drenched in sweat. Yet none of this had anything to do with how he got his name.

During his first week at Camp Green Lake, close to three years before, a scorpion had stung him on the arm, and the pain had traveled upward and settled in his armpit. It had felt like there was a hot needle twisting around inside him. He'd made the mistake of complaining about how much his armpit hurt. The pain eventually went away, but the name stuck.

"Theodore!" called his boss, Jack Dunlevy, a white man in his late thirties. "There's someone who would like to meet you."

Armpit stopped digging as his boss and a woman approached. The woman wore blue jeans and a loose-fitting white shirt. Her long silver hair was pulled back in a ponytail. Austin had a reputation for being a little weird, and the mayor fit right in.

"This is Theodore Johnson," said his boss.

Cherry Lane extended her hand. "How ya doin', Theodore?"

Armpit stood a head taller than the mayor. He had broad shoulders and thick muscular arms. At one time in his life he had been a little overweight, but all his digging and sweating had long since burned away any excess fat.

"Just fine," he said as he wiped his dirty hand on his shorts. "Sorry, I'm kind of sweaty."

"That's all right," the mayor said, and shook his hand.

Afraid of his own strength, Armpit tried not to grip the elderly woman's hand too hard, and was a little taken aback by the firmness of her handshake.

"I read all about the terrible things that went on at Camp Green Lake," she told him. "I want you to know that I admire you for getting through it and turning your life around."

Armpit wasn't sure what to say. "I admire what you've done for Austin."

He really had no idea what she'd done for the city. He knew she was supposed to be a strong environmentalist, but he'd heard his dad complain on several occasions that the "tree-huggers" only seemed to care about west Austin, an area well known for its rolling hills, nature preserves, and hike and bike trails. Most African Americans, including Armpit's family, lived in the flatlands of east Austin.

A mosquito buzzed by his ear, and he swatted at it. At least there hadn't been mosquitoes at Green Lake. It was too dry.

He had been sent to Camp Green Lake because of a bucket of popcorn. He had been trying to ease his way along a row of seats at the movies. He was only fourteen at the time, and was making his way past a couple of high school seniors when one of them stuck out his foot. They yelled at him for spilling popcorn on them, and he demanded that they pay for the popcorn, and by the time it was all over, the two older boys were in the hospital, and he was on his way to Camp Green Lake Juvenile Correctional Facility.

The name Green Lake was a cruel joke. He spent fourteen months in a dried-up lake bed, where he did nothing except dig holes. Later, when he applied for a job at Raincreek,

Jack Dunlevy warned him the job would require a fair bit of digging. Armpit just smiled and said, "No sweat."

After leaving Camp Green Lake, he first spent six months at a halfway house in San Antonio, where he attended school and received counseling. There were sixteen boys at the halfway house. The counselor there told them that the recidivism rate for African American boys was seventy-three percent. That meant, according to the statistics, that eleven or twelve of them would be arrested again before they turned eighteen. The counselor said the rate was even higher if you didn't finish high school.

"If you think life was unfair before you went to prison," she told Armpit, "it's going to be twice as bad when you go back. People are going to expect the worst from you, and will treat you that way."

She said his life would be like walking upstream in a rushing river. The secret was to take small steps and just keep moving forward. If he tried to take too big a step, the current would knock him off his feet and carry him back downstream.

Upon returning to Austin, he set five goals for himself. Five small steps. 1. Graduate from high school. 2. Get a job. 3. Save his money. 4. Avoid situations that might turn violent. And 5. Lose the name Armpit.

He picked up his shovel and went back to his trench.

Jack Dunlevy always brought a radio to the work site, and it was now playing a song by Kaira DeLeon.

I'm gonna take you for a ride,
And we're gonna have some fun!

The mayor, who had started to walk away, came hurrying back. "Oh, I love this song!" she exclaimed.

I'm gonna take you for a ride,
Ooh, and we're gonna have some fun!

Cherry Lane raised her arms in the air as she wiggled to the music. Armpit tried not to laugh. At least there was music. There had been no radios to listen to when he was digging holes at Camp Green Lake.

I'm gonna take you someplace
you never been before,
And you'll never be the same again!

2

A rusted Honda Civic drove noisily down the street and parked across from the mayor's house. Armpit had finished digging his trench and was attaching PVC pipe. The mayor had gone back inside.

The driver-side door had been bashed in, and it would have cost more to fix than the car was worth. The driver had to work his way over the stick shift and then exit on the passenger side.

The personalized license plate read: X RAY.

"Armpit!" X-Ray shouted as he crossed the street. "Armpit!"

The guys at work didn't know him by that name, but if he didn't say something X-Ray would just keep on shouting. Better to answer and shut him up.

"Hey," he called back.

"Man, you're really sweating," X-Ray said as he came near.

"Yeah, well, you'd sweat too if you were digging."

"I've already dug enough dirt to last one lifetime," said X-Ray.

They had met each other at Camp Green Lake.

"Look, don't call me Armpit around other people, all right?" Armpit said.

"But that's your name, dawg. You should never be ashamed of who you are."

X-Ray had the kind of smile that kept you from hating him no matter how annoying he was. He was skinny and wore glasses, which were now covered with clip-on shades.

He picked up Armpit's shovel. "Different shape."

"Yeah, it's for digging trenches, not holes."

X-Ray studied it awhile. "Seems like it would be harder to dig with. No leverage." He let it drop. "So you must be making a ton of money."

Armpit shrugged. "I'm doing all right."

"A ton of money," X-Ray repeated.

Armpit felt uncomfortable talking about money with X-Ray.

"So really, how much you got saved up so far?"

"I don't know. Not that much."

He knew exactly how much he had. Eight hundred and fifty-seven dollars. He hoped to break a thousand with his next paycheck.

"Got to be at least a thousand," said X-Ray. "You've been working for three months."

"Just part-time."

Besides working, Armpit was also taking two classes in summer school. He had to make up for all the schooling he'd missed while at Green Lake.

"And they take out for taxes and stuff, so really I don't take home all that much."

"Eight hundred?"

"I don't know, maybe."

"The reason I'm asking," X-Ray said, "the reason I'm asking is I got a business proposition for you. How would you like to double your money in less than two weeks?"

Armpit smiled as he shook his head. "I don't think so."

"I just need six hundred dollars. Double your money, guaranteed. And I won't be taking out any taxes."

"Look, things are going all right for me right now, and I just want to keep it all cool."

"Don't you even want to hear me out?"

"Not really."

"It's not against the law," X-Ray assured him. "I checked."

"Yeah, you didn't think selling little bags of parsley for fifty dollars an ounce was against the law either."

"Hey, it's not my fault what people *think* they're buying. How is that my fault? Am I supposed to be a mind reader?"

X-Ray had been sent to Camp Green Lake for selling bags of dried parsley and oregano to customers who thought they were buying marijuana. That was also why his family had to move from Lubbock to Austin shortly after he was released.

"Look, I just don't want to do anything that might screw things up," Armpit said.

"That's what you think? That I came here to screw things up? Man, I'm offering you an opportunity. An opportunity. If the Wright brothers came to you, you would have told them it's impossible to fly."

"*The Wright brothers?*" asked Armpit. "What century are you living in?"

"I just don't get it," said X-Ray. "I don't get it. I offer my best friend an opportunity to double his money, and he won't even listen to my idea."

"All right, tell me your idea."

"Forget it. If you're not interested I'll find somebody else."

"Tell me your idea." He actually was beginning to get just a little bit curious.

"What's the point?" asked X-Ray. "If you're not going to even listen . . ."

"All right, I'm listening," said Armpit.

X-Ray smiled. "Just two words." He paused for effect. "Kaira DeLeon."

It was eleven-thirty in Austin, but it was an hour later in Atlanta, where Kaira DeLeon, a seventeen-year-old African American girl, was just waking up. Her face pressed against

Pillow, which was, in fact, a pillow. There wasn't much oomph left in the stuffing, and the edges were frayed. The picture of the bear with a balloon, which had once been brightly colored, had faded so much it was hardly visible.

Kaira groggily climbed out of bed. She wore boxer shorts and was unbuttoning her pajama top as she made her way to what she thought was the bathroom. She opened the door, then shrieked. A thirty-year-old white guy, sitting on a couch, stared back at her. She clutched the two halves of her pajama top together and slammed the door.

The door bounced back open.

"Doofus!" Kaira shouted at the man, then closed the door again, making sure it latched this time. "Can't a person have some privacy around here!" she screamed, then made her way to the bathroom, which was on the opposite side of her bed.

Over the last three and a half weeks she'd been in nineteen different hotel suites, each with no fewer than three rooms, and one with six. So really, it was no wonder she went through the wrong door. She didn't even remember what city she was in.

She suspected that Polly, her psychiatrist, would tell her she had done that on purpose; something about wanting to show her body to her bodyguard. Maybe she was better off not telling Polly about it. Everything she said in her therapy sessions was supposed to be confidential, but Kaira suspected that Polly, like a parrot, repeated everything to El Genius.

Barnes & Noble Booksellers #2247
2200 Eastridge Loop Space 1420
San Jose, CA 95122
408-270-9470

STR:2247 REG:006 TRN:7571 CSHR:Elaine F

Small Steps
9780385733151
(1 @ 8.99)   8.99

Subtotal   8.99
Sales Tax (9.250%)   0.83

With a sales receipt, a full refund in the original form of payment will be issued from any Barnes & Noble store for returns of new and unread books (except textbooks) and unopened music/DVDs/audio made within (i) 14 days of purchase from a Barnes & Noble retail store (except for purchases made by check less than 7 days prior to the date of return) or (ii) 14 days of delivery date for Barnes & Noble.com purchases (except for purchases made via PayPal). A store credit for the purchase price will be issued for (i) purchases made by check less than 7 days prior to the date of return, (ii) when a gift receipt is presented within 60 days of purchase, (iii) textbooks returned with a receipt within 14 days of purchase, or (iv) original purchase was made through Barnes & Noble.com via PayPal. Opened music/DVDs/audio may not be returned, but can be exchanged only for the same title if defective.

After 14 days or without a sales receipt, returns or exchanges will not be permitted.

She had no privacy—not in her hotel room, not even in her own thoughts.

The problem was that, except for Polly, there wasn't anybody on the tour she could talk to. Certainly not her mother. And not her doofus bodyguard. The guys in her band were all at least forty years old, and treated her like she was a snot-nosed little kid. The backup singers were in their late twenties, but they seemed to resent her being the center of attention.

The only time she felt at peace was when she was singing. Then it was just her and the song and everybody else just disappeared.

Her concert tour would take her to a total of fifty-four cities, so she wasn't even half done yet. She was now on the southern swing. From Atlanta they'd be going to Jacksonville, then Miami, Birmingham, Memphis, Nashville, Little Rock, and Baton Rouge, and on to Texas: Houston, Austin, and Dallas. Originally the tour was supposed to include San Antonio instead of Austin, but that was changed at the last minute due to a monster truck rally at the Alamodome—not that Kaira cared, or even knew about the change.

Other people took care of things like that. Other people took care of everything. Kaira had accidentally left Pillow behind in New Haven, and Aileen, the tour's travel coordinator, took a flight back to Connecticut and personally searched the hotel laundry until she found it.

Kaira emerged from the bathroom thirty minutes later wearing a hotel robe. She called room service and ordered a glass of orange juice, pancakes, a cappuccino, and French fries. It would have to last her until the concert. If she tried to eat before the concert she'd puke. After a concert she usually had a bowl of ice cream.

She got dressed, then stepped back out to the sitting area. Fred, her doofus bodyguard, was still there, going through her mail.

"As soon as I turn eighteen, you're going to be the second person I fire."

Fred didn't even look up. It wasn't the first time he'd heard it.

The television was on CNN. Kaira changed the station to the Cartoon Network.

The first person she'd fire would be El Genius. He was her business manager and agent, and also happened to be married to her mother. They had gotten married shortly before the tour. His real name was Jerome Paisley, but he actually wanted people to call him El Genius. No matter how hard Kaira tried to sound sarcastic when she used that name, he always took it as a compliment.

Her father had been killed in Iraq. His name was John Spears. Kaira's real name was Kathy Spears, but there was already a famous singer with that last name.

El Genius had come up with the name Kaira DeLeon.

"You mean like Ponce de León?" Kaira had asked him.

"Who?"

Some genius.

Kaira explained to *the genius* who Ponce de León was, which was why her first CD was titled *The Fountain of Youth*. El Genius thought it looked classy for DeLeon to be spelled as one word, with a capital letter in the middle.

Kaira had learned all about Ponce de León when she was in fourth grade and living at the Pensacola Naval Air Station. She had to learn the history of Florida. By year's end she was living at Fort Myer, where they'd been studying the history of Virginia all year. She had never spent an entire school year in the same place.

"So, anything from Billy Boy?" she asked Fred.

Fred shook his head.

"Aw, too bad," Kaira said. "He writes such charming letters."

"It's not funny," said Fred.

"I think it's hilarious," said Kaira. She sang, "*Oh, where have you been, Billy Boy, Billy Boy? Oh, where have you been, charming Billy?*"

Billy Boy had sent her four letters so far. He told her he thought she was lovely, she sang like a bird, and someday he would kill her.

El Genius hired Fred after the first letter. Kaira wouldn't have been surprised if El Genius had actually written the letters, to scare her into staying confined to her hotel room.

He was such a control freak. She was sure Fred told him everything she did.

"You got another marriage proposal," Fred said.

"White or black?"

A photograph had been sent with the letter. Fred looked at it. "White," he said.

"What is it with you guys?" asked Kaira.

It was her seventh proposal, and every one had been from a white man.

Fred carefully put the letter and the photograph in a plastic bag.

"What are you doing that for?"

"FBI."

"He said he wanted to marry me, not kill me," Kaira pointed out.

"For some people, it's the same thing," said Fred.

Kaira glanced at him, surprised. The Doofus had actually said something kind of profound.

"Let me see what he looks like?"

Fred handed her the plastic bag.

Kaira laughed when she saw the picture. "He looks like you!" The photograph was that of a very muscular man wearing no shirt. The only difference between him and Fred was that his hair was long and wavy, while Fred had a buzz cut.

"You ought to grow your hair out," Kaira told him as she handed the plastic bag back to him.

Seven marriage proposals, and she'd never had a boyfriend.

◆ ◆ ◆

"Okay, here's the deal," said X-Ray. "Here's the deal. They just added Austin to her tour because of some kind of screwup in San Antonio. Tickets go on sale day after tomorrow. Fifty-five dollars a pop."

"Fifty-five dollars for just one ticket? I don't think so."

"In Philadelphia two front-row seats sold for seven hundred fifty dollars. Each."

Armpit couldn't believe it. "Seven hundred and fifty—"

"Each," X-Ray repeated.

"She's got a nice voice," said Armpit. "Kind of sassy, and playful, you know? You can always tell it's her."

X-Ray looked at him like he was crazy. "I don't want a critique! I want six hundred dollars." He spoke as if to somebody else. "He gives me a critique. Now he's a critic."

"Well, if I didn't think she could sing, I wouldn't give you six hundred dollars."

"So you're going to give me the money?"

He was considering it.

"See, here's the deal," X-Ray explained. "They only let you buy six tickets. So together we can buy twelve. Six hundred and sixty dollars. I've already got sixty, so I just need the rest from you. You won't have to do a thing. I'll do all the work. Then we'll split the profits."

Armpit slowly exhaled. "Six hundred dollars," he said.

"You'll make that back on one ticket," said X-Ray.

"No one's going to pay six hundred dollars for a ticket."

"They paid seven hundred and fifty in Philadelphia."

15

Armpit picked up his shovel and began filling in the dirt around the pipe.

"Okay, let's say we only sell the tickets for two hundred," said X-Ray. "After three tickets you get your money back. I won't get any of that. Then I get my sixty back out of the next ticket, and we split the rest right down the middle. So really there's no risk to you at all. You know we can sell three tickets."

Armpit replaced the sod, stomping it down with his boot.

"Think of it this way. It's like someone is offering to pay you to stand in line for him. What if your boss says to you, he says, 'Armpit, instead of digging today, I want you to stand in line for me, and I'll pay you a thousand bucks to do it.' Wouldn't you do it?"

"Of course."

"Same thing!" X-Ray said. "Some dudes are going to pay us a thousand bucks to stand in line for them. We just don't know who they are yet. See, you got to think outside the box."

A siren blared over the radio.

"Oh! Oh!" X-Ray exclaimed as he fumbled for the cell phone attached to his belt.

The siren noise had been made by an electric guitar, which slowly wound down and transformed into a flurry of notes and chords. It was the intro to Kaira DeLeon's biggest hit.

I hear a w-w-warning sound
Every time you c-c-come around.
Should you ch-chance to glance at me,
Threatens my security.

"C'mon, c'mon," X-Ray said into his phone.

Red Alert!
My hands are sh-sh-shakin'.
Red Alert!
Stomach's achin'.
Red Alert!
The earth beneath my f-f-feet is quakin'.

"Yeah—no, wait!" X-Ray said into the phone. "Just wait a sec—"

He scowled as he returned his phone to his belt. "Sixth," he griped. "Can you believe it? Sixth! Fifth caller gets two free tickets. Man, I hate this phone. The speed dial is too slow. How you supposed to compete with those rich white kids who have newer phones?"

"Too bad," said Armpit.

"That woulda been at least another four hundred for us," X-Ray said.

"For us?"

"Sure man, we're partners now, right?"

Armpit considered this question seriously. If he gave the

money to X-Ray, at least he'd still have two hundred and fifty-seven dollars left.

"Right?" X-Ray asked again.

> *Red Alert!*
> *My head is filled with a s-s-siren sound!*
> *Red Alert!*
> *All systems are shutting d-d-d-down!*

"Yeah, we're partners," Armpit agreed.

X-Ray patted him on the shoulder. "You won't regret it."

He already did.

3

Interstate 35 goes from the Mexican border all the way up to Lake Superior, and some of the heaviest traffic is along the two-hundred-fifty-mile stretch between San Antonio and Dallas. The steady flow of cars and trucks divides the city of Austin in half, not just geographically, but also economically, and to some extent, racially.

Armpit's home was in east Austin. The house was a duplex, with two identical front doors that faced each other across a wide front porch, 141A and 141B. Armpit's family lived in 141B. It was just him and his parents. He had an older sister who was married and lived in Houston, and an older brother serving eight to ten at Huntsville.

A white woman and her ten-year-old daughter, Ginny McDonald, occupied the other half of the house.

"S-s-six hun-did d-dollahs?" said Ginny. She was small for her age, with skinny arms and legs. She wore glasses that were so thick it was a wonder they could stay up on her tiny button nose.

"Hundred," said Armpit.

Ginny concentrated. "Hun-dred," she said. "That's a lot of m-money."

"Tell me about it," said Armpit.

They were walking around the block. Ginny's left hand kept holding on to, then letting go of Armpit. Her right arm was bent at the elbow, and rigidly upright, although she wasn't aware of it.

"Relax your arm," Armpit reminded her.

Ginny glanced at her arm as if it was a separate being from herself. It took a moment for her brain to send the proper signals, and then her arm lowered.

She reminded Armpit of a marionette who was also her own puppeteer. She had to figure out which string to pull to make her arms and legs move properly.

She had been born with cerebral palsy. A few neighborhood kids called her spaz, and retard, but most treated her with respect because she was a friend of Armpit's, and because she was willing to answer their questions.

"What's wrong with you?" someone might ask.

If there was a taunt in the question she never noticed. "I had bleeding inside my brain wh-when I was born."

And that seemed to satisfy whoever asked the question.

She and her mother had moved into their half of the

duplex when Armpit was still at Camp Green Lake. Her mother was ready to move away when she found out that the boy next door was a violent criminal who would soon be returning home.

She was now glad she hadn't.

Ginny and Armpit hit it off from the beginning. She didn't fear him, and he didn't pity her.

Not long after they started their daily walks, Ginny stopped wearing her leg braces, claiming they pinched her. She had a walker as well, but only used that if she needed to move quickly, like at school when they went outside for recess.

But as much as Armpit helped her, she helped him even more. She gave his life meaning. For the first time in his life, there was someone who looked up to him, who cared about him.

Together they were learning to take small steps.

"She s-sings like I talk," said Ginny.

"How do you mean?"

"*H-hands are sh-sh-shaking!*" sang Ginny.

Armpit laughed. "You know that's just part of the song," he said.

"Yes. But I l-like it."

"Me too," said Armpit. "So if you had the money, would you pay fifty-five dollars for a ticket?"

"Yes."

"How about seventy-five?"

"Yes."

"A hundred?"

"No."

He laughed. "They paid seven hundred and fifty dollars in Philadelphia."

"No way!" said Ginny.

"That's what X-Ray said."

"You c-can't believe everything X-Ray s-says."

She was right about that.

"You sweat a lot." With just one finger extended, she delicately touched a large circle of sweat under his arm.

"Yeah, well, it's hot out."

"I don't sweat," said Ginny.

"You will when you get older."

"And I will w-walk and t-talk better."

"Yes, you will," said Armpit. "But sweating's got nothing to do with your disability. It's just because you haven't reached puberty yet."

Ginny giggled.

"What's so funny?"

"You s-said puberty."

Armpit laughed too, not at the word, but at her reaction to it.

Ginny was still laughing as they headed up the cracked driveway to their shared house. Weeds poked up through the broken cement.

"What are you two laughing at?" asked Ginny's mother, who had come out to the front porch.

"Something," said Ginny.

Armpit winked at her.

Ginny tried to wink back. She closed and opened both her eyes together.

Even though the two families lived inside it, the house was smaller than most of the homes in west Austin where Armpit planted shrubs and installed irrigation systems. An oak tree in the front yard shaded almost the entire house.

There were few trees this size in west Austin. That half of the city was mostly built on solid white limestone, with only a little bit of topsoil above it. Dirt had to be trucked in whenever Raincreek Irrigation and Landscaping planted anything.

According to Armpit's father, the cost of air-conditioning the homes in west Austin, with their high ceilings and grand entrances, was greater than the amount he paid in rent.

Armpit's father worked in the daytime as a meter reader for the electric company. At night he was a dispatcher for a taxicab company. Armpit's mother worked as a checker for H-E-B, a local supermarket chain.

Armpit said good-bye to Ginny and her mother, then went inside. His parents were in the kitchen chopping vegetables.

"Hey, how're things goin'?" his father called.

"They're goin'," Armpit muttered as he continued down the hall.

"Hold on, I want to talk to you," said his father.

Armpit sighed. "What about?"

"Just come here."

Armpit stepped into the kitchen. "Look, I been working all afternoon and I'm hot and dirty and sweaty. Can't a person just take a shower without going through the third degree?"

"No one's accusing you of anything," said his mother. "Your dad hardly gets to see you since he started working for Yellow Cab."

"Fine, now you can see me," Armpit said.

"I don't appreciate your attitude," said his father.

"Sorry, I'll change my attitude," Armpit said. "Whatever that means."

"What's wrong with your eyes?" his mother asked him.

"There's nothing wrong with my eyes. I'm tired."

"How you get home?" his father asked.

"Hernandez."

"I want a sample," his father said.

"Why, because he's Mexican? Actually, we were working at the mayor's house. Maybe you think I got stoned with the mayor?"

His mother laughed. "I wouldn't put it past her."

"The mayor shook my hand," Armpit said. "She said she admired me."

"What'd she mean by that?" asked Armpit's mother.

"You know. Working hard, goin' to school. She'd read about Green Lake."

"And how does she know you were at Green Lake?" his mother asked.

"I guess my boss told her."

"That's supposed to be confidential," his mother said. "Those records are supposed to be sealed."

"It's no big secret! Everybody at school knows."

"And that's supposed to make me feel better?"

"I give up!" Armpit said.

Most parents would be proud if the mayor said she admired their son!

"I want a sample," his father repeated.

"Why, because I'm tired after working all day?"

"No, because you're being very defensive. If you've got nothing to hide . . ."

Armpit marched off to the bathroom, where he got a plastic cup out from under the sink.

After he returned from Camp Green Lake, his parents bought a home drug-testing kit. They weren't going to stand by and let him ruin his life, like his brother. He had tried pointing out that the reason he'd been sent to Green Lake had nothing to do with drugs or alcohol, but that didn't make any difference to them.

"Drugs and alcohol can lead to violence," his mother had said.

So could a bucket of popcorn.

4

Armpit showered again in the morning, dried off, then ran a stick of deodorant three times under each armpit. He splashed his face with aftershave lotion. He only shaved every other day, but he put on aftershave lotion every day.

There was a girl in his speech class who smiled at him a lot lately. Her name was Tatiana.

He sprayed Sploosh on his feet. He didn't have a problem with foot odor, but when your name was Armpit you had to be extra careful. He sprayed some Sploosh under each armpit for extra protection.

One of the guys from Camp Green Lake had sent him a whole case of Sploosh. It was probably meant as a joke, but the guy's father had invented the stuff, so maybe not.

The phone was ringing when he stepped out of the bathroom. It was X-Ray.

"Hey, partner. You know the six hundred dollars?"

"Yeah, I'm going to stop by the ATM after school."

"Good. Only you need to make it six hundred and sixty."

"I thought you were putting up sixty," Armpit reminded him.

"I am," said X-Ray. "I am. The thing is, there's a five-dollar service charge on each ticket. So even though the tickets are fifty-five dollars, they cost sixty."

That made no sense at all.

"Better make it an even seven hundred," said X-Ray. "Just in case."

Seven hundred. That would leave him with only a hundred and fifty-seven dollars. A hundred and fifty-seven dollars after three months of working.

"That's not a problem, is it?"

"No. No problem," said Armpit.

"You'll still double your money," X-Ray assured him. "Guaranteed. So really, you'll be making more money this way."

Despite all his efforts, he was sticky with sweat after walking the five blocks from home to school. At eight-fifty-five in the morning the temperature was already in the mid-eighties, and the humidity made it seem even hotter.

Tatiana had her back to him when he entered the room.

She was talking to her friend Claire. Tatiana had two long braids, which actually connected at the tips, forming a giant V. He'd never seen any other girl wear her hair that way, but everything about Tatiana was a little bit goofy. That was what he liked about her. That, and the fact that she smiled at him.

"Hey, Tatiana," he said, trying to sound casual, but he was too casual and she didn't hear him. He said it again, a little louder and more abruptly.

She turned. "What?"

"Uh, nothing. Just wanted to say hi."

"Hi," she said, but without the smile.

Speech class always made him nervous even when there was no speech due. Coach Simmons sometimes called on students to speak extemporaneously. Armpit had a fear of standing at the front of the room, not knowing what to say, sweating, as Tatiana stared at him. He had a hard enough time even when he'd prepared a speech.

Fortunately, there were no extemporaneous speeches this day. Most of the class period was spent discussing the next major assignment. Everyone had to bring a stuffed animal to school and give a campaign speech for it. Then there would be an election to see which stuffed animal would be elected ruler of the world.

"I don't even have a stuffed animal," Armpit said aloud as he walked out of the classroom.

There was a laugh, with just a little bit of a snort mixed with it. "You are so funny," Tatiana said, touching his arm.

He didn't even know she was there, and hadn't tried to be funny, but he was glad she thought he was.

"I hear you're going out for football next year," she said.

"No, I just wanted Coach Simmons to think that. He gives better grades to football players."

"So you lied to him?" asked Tatiana. "Isn't that kind of cheating?"

Armpit shrugged.

How could it be cheating? It was unfair that the coach gave better grades to football players, and he was just trying to even things out. However, by the time he put those thoughts together Tatiana had already walked away.

His other class was economics. Armpit liked Mr. Warren, a bald-headed white guy, but he had trouble understanding all the graphs. Somehow by looking at the graphs he was supposed to be able to tell what would happen to the price of a cup of coffee if there was a drought in Brazil. It made about as much sense to him as a fifty-five-dollar ticket costing sixty dollars.

Part of his problem was that half the stuff Mr. Warren talked about had nothing to do with the assignments.

"I have here a ten-dollar bill," Mr. Warren said, taking it out of his wallet and holding in the air for all to see. "I'll sell it to the highest bidder. Do I hear fifty cents?"

Armpit wasn't quite sure what he meant by that, and he wasn't the only one. Most of the class seemed confused, but then Matt Kapok, a kid in the front row, offered fifty cents.

"Going once, going twice—"

"Wait a second," said the girl who sat next to Armpit. "You mean you're going to sell your ten-dollar bill to Matt for fifty cents?"

"Yep," said Mr. Warren. "Unless I get a better offer."

"Sure, I'll give you sixty cents for it," said the girl.

Someone else offered seventy-five cents, then a dollar, and before too long it was up to nine dollars and ninety-nine cents. And then someone bid ten dollars, trading his ten-dollar bill for Mr. Warren's.

There was a lesson in all that, but Armpit wasn't quite sure exactly what it was.

"One year I actually sold it for ten dollars and ten cents," Mr. Warren told the class.

Eighteen hundred miles away, Kaira DeLeon was getting her own lesson in economics.

"I just want to know how much money I made so far," she said.

"It's not that simple, dear," said her mother.

"I'm not asking *you*," said Kaira.

Her mother had on an aqua and indigo silk jacket, with a small sapphire pinned to the lapel. Kaira hadn't seen either the jacket or the pin before, but that wasn't surprising. Her mother seemed to show up with a new outfit daily.

"I can't give you exact figures," said Jerome Paisley, Kaira's agent and business manager.

He had just returned from the hotel's health club, and

30

was still wearing his running shorts and a V-neck undershirt. A gold chain hung around his thick neck.

He had a large forehead and a puffy face, which was no doubt the result of taking steroids. At one time he'd been a pro baseball player, although, except for eighteen days, he'd never made it out of the minor leagues. His career was ruined after he was hit in the face by a pitch.

Kaira always wondered how someone could get hit in the face by a pitch. *You have to see it coming, don't you?*

"Have I made a million dollars yet?" she asked.

"There are a lot of expenses. Do you even know how many people are on this tour?"

She was too embarrassed to say she didn't, so she remained silent.

"Forty-two," said Jerome Paisley. "Everyone gets salaries, per diems, travel expenses. And then there are additional costs associated with each venue."

"What's my salary?"

"You don't get a salary. You get what's left over after everyone else is paid."

"You're doing very well, sweetie," said her mother.

"How much does the Doofus get paid?" Kaira asked.

"I've asked you not to call him that," said her mother.

"I just want to know. How much do you have to pay a babysitter?"

"Fred gets fourteen hundred a week, plus expenses," said her business manger, her mother's husband.

Kaira laughed. "And what about your new jacket?" she asked her mother. "Who paid for that?"

"Your money all goes into a trust account," said her mother's husband. "Nobody can touch it, not even your mother. You'll get it when you turn eighteen."

"Yeah, well, a lot is going to happen when I turn eighteen," Kaira said.

If Jerome Paisley heard the threat, he chose not to acknowledge it. "It doesn't really matter even if you don't make a dime on this tour," he told her. "Right now, it's all about exposure. Getting your name out there. Getting your songs on the radio. You'll make more money in CD sales than you'll ever make on the tour."

"Maybe we should charge more for the tickets," Kaira suggested.

"Oh, you think so?"

She didn't like his patronizing tone.

"In Philadelphia, tickets went for seven hundred and fifty dollars," she said, trying to show that she knew a thing or two.

"Where'd you hear that?"

"I don't know," Kaira said, suddenly feeling defensive. "On the radio, I think."

He smirked at her. "I planted that story," he boasted. "You didn't even sell out in Philly." He pointed to his big, fat head and said, "El Genius at work."

Kaira felt foolish.

"The most important thing in this business isn't talent," he told her. "It's all about hype. Hype and buzz."

"Well, it still makes me mad that ticket scalpers make the money instead of me."

"You let me worry about the business end of things. You just keep singing and shaking that sexy little body."

"Listen to what Jerome tells you," said Kaira's mother. She gave her husband a kiss on his puffy cheek. "He's made you what you are."

5

X-Ray picked Armpit up at four o'clock in the morning, and they drove to the Lonestar Arena. "Anything in the first row is pure gold," he said. "Pure gold. The second row too. Anything in the first two rows."

Armpit brought his economics book along. He knew he'd probably miss speech, but there was a test in econ and he couldn't afford to miss that.

When they pulled into the parking lot, they saw that a line had already formed at the ticket window. Tickets wouldn't go on sale until eight o'clock.

"Man, I told you we should have spent the night here," X-Ray said.

"You never said that."

"Well, I thought it."

They got in line. There were already twenty-nine people ahead of them in line. X-Ray counted it twice.

Armpit lay on his back in the gravel parking lot with his eyes closed. His economics book was his pillow. He planned to study when there was enough light. A piece of gravel dug into his back, but the more he tried to smooth it out the worse it got, so he did his best to ignore it.

Somebody in line had brought a boom box, and *The Fountain of Youth*, Kaira DeLeon's CD, was playing. Armpit was lying there, his eyes closed, only half listening, when he suddenly heard her sing:

> *These shoes, these jewels, this dress,*
> *A perfect picture of success.*
> *Oh, you would never guess, Armpit,*
> *A damsel in distress.*

At least, that was what it sounded like.

> *Save me, Armpit!*
> *A damsel in distress.*

He sat up. "Did you hear that?"

"Hear what?" asked X-Ray.

"Never mind."

If he told him, X-Ray would never let him live it down.

Why would she sing "Armpit"? It was impossible. There was no possible way. He must have fallen asleep for a second and dreamed it.

In line behind them were five men who seemed especially dirty and ragged. Armpit might have guessed they were street people, except for the fact that they were waiting in line to buy sixty-dollar tickets. From the way they smelled, he thought maybe they worked for the sanitation department and had come here after work.

"I'm thinking third row," X-Ray said. "Third or fourth. As long as we're somewhere in the first five rows we're golden."

Armpit looked at the people in line ahead of him. Nearly all were white, even though Kaira DeLeon was African American. Several wore shirts and ties.

"I don't know," he said. "If everybody buys six tickets—"

"Not everyone's going to buy six tickets," X-Ray interrupted. "Besides, you really don't want to be too close. It's better to be a few rows back. The best seats are between row three and row seven. Those are the ones that will bring in the big money."

Shortly after sunrise, Armpit opened his book and tried to understand the difference between fixed costs and variable costs. Graphs illustrated how these changed as more goods were produced. The line representing fixed costs was flat, and the one representing variable costs angled upward.

It might as well have been written in Chinese.

"Look at all the people behind us!" X-Ray pointed out. "They'd pay a hundred dollars just to have our place in line."

"I'll take it," said Armpit.

X-Ray laughed. "We're going to make a lot more than that, my friend. A lot more."

After a while a guy wearing a Lonestar Arena T-shirt came out and tried to adjust the line so that instead of sticking straight out from the ticket window, it went parallel to the building. This caused a lot of grumbling from the grubby guys sitting behind Armpit.

"What difference does it make?"

"I was just gettin' comfortable."

"Just because you got the T-shirt doesn't make you God!"

But they got up and moved along with everyone else.

The mystery of who they were was solved shortly after seven-thirty, when the guys who were paying them showed up. One was a fast-talking, skinny white guy. With him was a big dude wearing a cowboy hat and boots.

"Now listen up, 'cause I'm not going to repeat myself," said the skinny guy. He wore a pearl earring and had a face that needed to make a choice—either shave or grow a beard. "When you get to the ticket window, Moses here will give you an envelope containing three hundred and thirty dollars. You don't have to count it. You just hand it to the ticket agent and ask for six tickets. You then give the tickets to Moses, and he will pay you twenty-five dollars."

"Twenty-five dollars!" complained one of the guys.

"We've been sitting here for five hours! I could make more than that sitting on the corner of Mopac and Spicewood."

"You want to go, go," said the skinny guy.

The big guy in the cowboy hat—Moses, apparently—had a thermos of coffee and a bag of breakfast tacos, which he handed out. He tried to give Armpit a taco.

"I'm not one of them," Armpit said, somewhat offended.

"We're not part of your crew," said X-Ray.

"Oh yeah?" said the skinny one. "Just a Kaira DeLeon fan, are you?"

"We're independent," said X-Ray.

"Well, we got a couple of extra tacos if you want 'em."

Armpit and X-Ray looked at each other, then happily took the tacos.

Moses filled a Styrofoam cup of coffee for X-Ray. Armpit didn't drink coffee.

"I'm Felix," said the skinny guy. "This is my man Moses."

"X-Ray," said X-Ray. "And that's my man Armpit."

"Armpit, huh?"

"A scorpion—"

"Tell you what," said Felix. "After you get your tickets, come talk to me."

"We're going to have to leave straight away," said Armpit. "I got an economics test."

"Listen to me, Armpit," said Felix. "I bring you a breakfast taco, the least you can do is talk to me. If you're studying econ, then you should know. There's no such thing as a free lunch."

◆ ◆ ◆

The ticket windows didn't open until ten after eight, and the line moved excruciatingly slowly.

"C'mon, c'mon. How long does it take to buy a ticket?" X-Ray yelled at the people in front of him.

There were two ticket windows. X-Ray went first, and when Armpit reached the one next to him, he could hear X-Ray arguing with the ticket agent. "Are you sure this is the best you got? Well, can you check?"

Armpit paid for his tickets. They were all in row M. He counted in his head. The thirteenth row. On the back of each ticket, printed in bold letters, were the words *This ticket may not be resold.*

"M's good," said X-Ray. "It's the first half of the alphabet. That's all that matters. Just look at all those fools still waiting in line!" He laughed. "They'll be lucky if they're in the same zip code."

Armpit pointed out what was written on the back of each ticket, but X-Ray wasn't concerned. "They can write anything they want. It doesn't mean squat. This is America. Everything's for sale."

They watched as Moses paid the last member of his crew.

"Those guys are so cool," X-Ray said. "That could be us in a few years."

Felix headed toward them. "So, X-Ray, you get good seats?"

"Row M!"

"M's good," said Felix. "First half of the alphabet."

39

"That's what I was tellin' Armpit."

"The first few rows are reserved for friends and radio stations. It's a rip-off, but what can you do?"

"What can you do?" X-Ray agreed.

"Tell you what. I'll give you seventy bucks for each ticket. That's fifteen more than face value. Times twelve, you'll make a hundred and eighty dollars. Ninety bucks each."

"They cost sixty, not fifty-five," said Armpit.

"Yeah I know," said Felix. "There's a five-dollar service charge. What a rip-off. But the thing is, you try to sell the tickets, and all the customer's gonna see is the face value."

"We're not interested," said X-Ray.

"All right, I'll pay the damn service charge. Seventy-five a ticket."

"We can do a lot better," said X-Ray.

"Maybe," Felix agreed. "Maybe you can. I'm not saying you can't. But you never know. A bird in the hand. Ninety dollars, Armpit, for just a morning's work. Hard to beat that."

"We're not interested," said X-Ray.

"Armpit looks interested. How about it, Armpit?"

It did sound pretty good to him. Ninety dollars was more than he made in two days of digging.

"They sold for seven hundred and fifty in Philly," said X-Ray.

"Austin ain't Philly," said Felix. "And row M ain't exactly the front row."

"We were ahead of your guys in line," said X-Ray. "Whatever we got has to be better than anything you got."

"Look, I'm not saying you couldn't make more than seventy-five dollars a ticket. I wouldn't be talkin' to you if I didn't think so. But there's risk, too. Right now, things are looking pretty good. Big demand. Short supply. The price can only go up. But there was a big demand when Dylan played here a few years back. So you know what they did? They added a second show. You're the economist, Armpit. You know what happens when supply goes up?"

"The price goes down?"

"Like an elevator with a busted cable. I was lucky to unload my inventory. Or what do you think would happen if we learn that sweet little Miss Kaira is pregnant? Or say she burns the American flag in some kind of political protest? I can tell you what would happen. You wouldn't be able to give your tickets away."

"Yeah, well, if it's so risky, then why do you want the tickets so badly?" asked X-Ray.

"This is my business. If I lose money on Kaira DeLeon, I'll make it up next week on someone else. You're going to have to put an ad in the paper. That costs money. Me, I already got a running ad. It costs me the same no matter how many tickets I'm selling."

"A fixed cost," Armpit said as it all suddenly made sense to him.

"And I got connections, too," Felix went on. "Every hotel concierge knows who to call if some guest wants tickets.

41

All I'm sayin' is, it's not as easy as you think for a couple of independents. I'm offering you a hundred and eighty dollars, pure profit, and no worries."

"We ain't worried," said X-Ray.

"Armpit looks worried."

"I'm cool," said Armpit.

Felix smiled. "Then why are you sweating so much?"

"Don't you worry. We're going to make a lot more than ninety bucks apiece," X-Ray assured him as they drove out of the parking lot. "A lot more. Felix wouldn'ta wanted to buy them if he didn't think so. This is a great day! We're on our way, partner! We are on our way!"

By the time they reached the high school, Armpit was already five minutes late for his test. As he was getting out of the car, X-Ray said, "By the way. I'm going to need thirty bucks to put an ad in the paper."

6

He was walking home from school an hour later when a man coming the other way crossed to the other side of the street. It was no big deal, and maybe the guy really needed to cross the street, but that kind of thing happened a lot to Armpit. White people did it more, but African Americans did it too. He usually pretended not to notice, but sometimes he'd give the guy a menacing glare as if to say, "Yeah, you better stay out of my way!"

This time he just ignored it. He was in too good a mood to glare.

He'd gotten a ninety on his economics test, thanks to Felix. He'd learned more in the parking lot of the Lonestar Arena than he had learned all year in class.

"It all just clicked," he told Ginny as they took their

daily walk. "Even the graphs! The questions were all about people buying and selling everything from gasoline to hula hoops, but in my own mind, I put it in terms of tickets."

"Hula hoops," Ginny said with a laugh. "That's funny!"

After their walk, he asked her if he could borrow a stuffed animal for his ruler-of-the-world speech.

Ginny was amazed. Hula hoops, stuffed animals, ruler of the world—high school sounded a lot more fun than the fourth grade.

She led him into her room, where she had more than thirty stuffed animals.

"Just give me one you don't like too much," Armpit said.

"I love all of them," Ginny said, but not in a selfish way. She definitely considered it an honor for one of her lovies to get to go to high school with Theodore, and she carefully considered who was most deserving.

"How about that one," Armpit said, indicating a brown owl with huge eyes.

"That's Hoo-Hooter," said Ginny. "He can't see."

"He can't?"

"He's blind. But he can h-hear really g-good and so he never b-bumps into trees."

"How can he hear trees?" Armpit asked.

"The leaves rustle in the wind," said Ginny.

Ginny must have said that same sentence many times before because she didn't stutter over any of the words.

"This is Daisy," she said, handing Armpit a basset hound with long, floppy ears.

"How ya doin', Daisy?" said Armpit.

"She c-can't hear you," said Ginny. "She's deaf. But she has a keen sense of smell."

Armpit smiled. He liked it that she used the word "keen."

The next one she showed him was Roscoe, a fuzzy bear with twisty arms and legs. Roscoe was paralyzed due to a "horrible accident."

Ginny sat on the edge of the bed with her legs bowed out and her toes pointed downward. As a baby she couldn't learn to walk because she was always on tiptoe. She had to wear a special brace just to straighten out her feet.

Armpit looked over the three animals. Hooter was out. Everyone would just laugh at the name.

"Oh, I know!" Ginny suddenly exclaimed as she brought both hands to her face. "You need Coo!"

Coo was a sort of bunny creature lying next to Ginny's bed. It had arms and legs like a person but had bunny ears.

"I've had Coo my whole life," Ginny said.

"I better just take Roscoe," said Armpit.

Ginny frowned.

"I think Coo's great," Armpit assured her. "I just don't want to take your favorite. It's just a stupid speech. What if something happens?"

"Coo isn't scared," said Ginny. "He is always strong and brave. H-he will be the b-best ruler of the w-w-world!"

"Well, I wouldn't count on Coo winning," Armpit cautioned. "I get real nervous when I have to give a speech."

"Coo will help you," said Ginny.

Armpit held Coo in one hand. It was soft and spongy, the kind of toy given to babies because it was easily held on to by tiny fingers. "So is there something wro—" He caught himself. "Does Coo have a disability?" he asked.

"Leukemia," Ginny whispered. "But we don't talk about it."

7

Friday, with the concert just eight days away, Armpit went to the Stop & Shop after school to buy a newspaper. He had paid thirty dollars for the ad; he might as well pay another fifty cents to see it.

He dropped two quarters into the newspaper vending machine and pulled up on the handle, but it wouldn't open. He pressed the coin return and got back nothing. He pulled harder on the handle. He slammed his hand against the coin return.

He was already mad that X-Ray had waited two days to buy the ad because he only wanted to pay for one week, and now the machine had eaten his money. He shook it so hard he might have broken it, but then a voice in his head reminded him that it wasn't worth going to jail for fifty cents.

Instead, he went into the store and told the clerk what had happened.

"You have to wait for the coins to drop," the guy told him, and wouldn't give him his money back.

Armpit asked him for change for a dollar.

"No change."

So he bought a bag of chips for a dollar and nineteen cents, then used part of the change to buy another paper.

This time he listened for each quarter to drop before pulling on the handle. When the door opened, he took three copies of the *Austin American Statesman*, just to get even, and left two of them on top of the machine.

Back home, he spread the classified ads out across the kitchen table. He'd told X-Ray not to ask for too much, since they only had a week. There were a number of ads for Kaira DeLeon tickets. The prices ranged from seventy-five to a hundred and ten dollars. Then he came to the one with X-Ray's phone number.

Kaira DeLeon Tkts. $135
Close to the front. 555–3470

X-Ray answered on the second ring.

"Are you insane?" Armpit shouted.

"Yes, but it hasn't stopped me before!"

"Did you see all the other ads in the paper?"

"Yeah, so?"

"So they're all at least twenty-five dollars cheaper."

"And your point is?"

"I told you to keep the price low."

"It is low. They sold for seven hundred and fifty in Philly."

"We're not going to be able to sell any tickets."

"You're thinking east Austin," said X-Ray. "You got to think west Austin."

"*What?*"

"See, you and me, we'd buy the cheapest tickets. But that's not how they think in west Austin. They don't worry about money over there. They just want the best. And the ones that cost the most got to be the best, right?"

Armpit had installed enough sprinkler systems in west Austin to know that people worried about money over there just as much as they did east of I-35. Their homes might have been worth half a million dollars, but they still expected Armpit's boss to reimburse them five bucks if Armpit accidentally stepped on a daffodil.

"Okay," Armpit said. "Even if somebody wanted to pay a little more to be up front," he said, "row M is *not* the front!"

"The ad doesn't say it's in the front. It says *close to* the front."

"It's not close to the front. Row F is close to the front. G maybe."

"So then they're *close to* close to the front," said X-Ray.

"Just call the paper and tell them to lower the price," said Armpit.

"You need to relax. I promised you I'd double your money, didn't I? Didn't I?"

Double or nothing, thought Armpit.

"Besides, it'll cost another ten bucks to change the ad."

He didn't sleep that night, or the next night, or the night after that. X-Ray didn't sell a single ticket over the weekend.

He wondered how he had ever let X-Ray talk him into this. Why didn't they sell the tickets to Felix when they had the chance? Now he was out another thirty dollars for the ad in the paper, and it would cost ten more to change it.

But at three o'clock Monday morning, he decided that was what they would have to do. Just change the ad. Seventy-five dollars. They'd still make a small profit. Maybe if they had gotten seats in the first or second row they could have held out for more money, but now they just needed to get rid of the tickets before it was too late.

At four o'clock in the morning he decided on seventy dollars a ticket.

"That's five dollars less than Felix offered!" X-Ray said when Armpit called him before going to school.

"Well, we should have sold them to Felix when we had the chance," Armpit said. "But we didn't, and now I just want to get the things sold."

"For seventy dollars?"

"We'll still come out ahead, even after the cost of the ad."

"So you don't want to sell them for a hundred and thirty-five?"

"That's what I said. Look, it's my money on the line."

"That's a problem," said X-Ray.

"I'll pay the ten dollars!"

"It's not that," said X-Ray. "It's just . . ."

"Now what?"

X-Ray heaved a heavy sigh. "Well, a guy just called and he wants to buy two tickets at a hundred and thirty-five. He's meeting me after he gets off work. I guess I'll just call him back and tell him they only cost seventy." He laughed. "I mean, if that's what you want me to do." He laughed again.

Armpit managed a smile.

Later at work he had to remove a red tip photinia from someone's yard, and its root was enormous. He first cut off the bush at the base, then started on the root, but no matter how deep he dug, he never could seem to get to the bottom of it. It was like an octopus with thick, long tentacles that hugged the ground.

He went at it with an axe, hacking off many of its offshoots, but to no avail. Finally he wrapped a chain around it and attached the other end to the back of a pickup truck.

He climbed into the cab, put it into four-wheel drive,

and shifted into first gear. There was a moment of uncertainty, and he worried he might destroy the engine, but then the root popped out of the ground.

He lifted it into the back of the pickup along with the top half of the bush. He was hot, tired, sore, and covered with dirt and sweat.

But he felt good. He had a feeling of satisfaction that he could never explain to X-Ray. It was good clean work. Scalping tickets felt dirty in comparison.

8

He and Ginny waited out front for X-Ray to bring the money from the ticket sales.

"Two hun-hundred and seventy dollars," said Ginny. "If you s-sell ten more . . ." She did the math aloud. "Ten times one hundred and thirty-five is one thousand three hundred and fifty!" Her eyes widened. "You're rich!"

Armpit laughed. "Well, I'll have to split the profits with X-Ray. When we sell all the tickets I'll make a profit of four hundred and thirty-five dollars." He had done the math too. "You know, you didn't stutter at all when you were adding," he pointed out.

"I only stutter when I t-t-t-talk."

"You were talking."

"That was math. I'm g-good with numbers. Not w-w-words."

"Well, you're pretty smart," he said.

"And you're pretty rich."

"And you're pretty cute."

"And you're pretty pretty."

She laughed at her own joke.

"What's so funny?"

"I s-said you were pretty."

"So?"

"G-girls are pretty. Boys are handsome. That m-means you're a girl!"

"And you're pretty silly," said Armpit.

He noticed a woman watching them from the parking lot of the Stop & Shop. He wondered if she was suspicious because he was with a little white girl. Did she think they were on drugs? Maybe she was memorizing his face, in case it turned out the girl had been abducted.

He stared back at the woman, who then quickly got into her car and drove away.

Or maybe she just enjoyed seeing two people smiling and laughing.

The X-Mobile passed her coming in the other direction.

"There's X-Ray," said Ginny.

Not bothering with a U-turn, X-Ray parked facing the wrong way. He slid over to the passenger side, climbed out, then walked around the car.

"Hey, Ginny. You taking good care of Armpit?"

"Yes."

"So, did you sell the tickets?" Armpit asked.

X-Ray smiled. "See, Ginny, that's what I like about Armpit. Straight to the point. No bull—" He stopped himself. "No bull."

"He d-doesn't like to be called Armpit."

"I mean it with great respect and affection," X-Ray said, his hand on his heart.

"Did you sell the tickets?" Armpit asked again.

"Say, Ginny, did I ever tell you what happened to my car?" X-Ray asked, pointing to the big gash in the driver-side door.

"No."

"I'm driving along Mopac, and this dinosaur leaps out and takes a big bite out of my door! Scared me half to death!"

Ginny laughed.

"Look, do you see the teeth marks?"

Ginny pushed back her glasses on her nose. "Yes."

"I think it was a T. rex! Can you believe it?"

"No."

X-Ray laughed.

"So you didn't sell the tickets, did you?" said Armpit.

"Okay, here's the deal," said X-Ray. I was supposed to meet the dude in the parking lot of the H-E-B at five-fifteen. Hey, Ginny, you know what H-E-B stands for?"

"No."

"Howard E. Butt. Seriously. That was the man's name.

That's why they just call it H-E-B. Would you want to buy your groceries at a place called Butt's?"

Ginny cracked up.

Armpit glared at X-Ray.

"Okay, so anyway," X-Ray continued, "I get there at five o'clock, fifteen minutes early. So then I wait. The guy said he'd be driving a white Suburban. Five-fifteen: no white Suburban. Five-twenty-five. Five-thirty. It's like a hundred and fifty degrees in the parking lot, but still I wait 'cause I don't want to let my buddy Armpit down. Finally, at five-thirty-five, I hear this guy screaming out, 'X-Ray! X-Ray!' like some kind of maniac. So I give a couple a toot-toots and then this obese vehicle pulls up beside me and two ol' rednecks get out. 'Are you X-Ray?'

"'No, I'm just some dude who happens to have X-Ray on his license plate'—but I don't say that. I say, 'Yeah, that's me,' and I'm just about to hand over the tickets when he asks, now get this, Ginny, he asks who he should make the check out to.

"I tell him he can make the check out to the tooth fairy for all I care. He goes into this whole riff about losing his ATM card, which was why he was late, but I don't want to hear it."

"So you didn't sell the tickets?" asked Armpit.

"They still want 'em," said X-Ray. "They're going to meet me back at the H-E-B at ten tonight. They say they'll have the cash this time. Only, you better come with."

"I can't. I got econ homework, a speech to write—man,

56

I thought you were supposed to do all the work. I just put up the money."

"They were two big white guys. And there won't be too many people around at ten o'clock. I just think it's a good idea to have some backup."

Armpit didn't like where this was heading.

"Don't worry. One look at you and there won't be any trouble."

For better or for worse, Armpit knew that was probably true.

He worked on his Coo speech until it was time to go, first making an outline, then putting his key points on three-by-five cards. His speech was mostly about Ginny and how important Coo was to her. He came up with a sentence he really liked: *Coo gives her comfort, courage, and confidence.*

He realized he might be taking the assignment a little too seriously. The people who had given their speeches earlier today had treated the election as if it was a big joke, which of course it was. One girl had urged everyone to vote for Milford the Monkey because if he became ruler of the world, he would plant a million banana trees, and that would stop the destruction of the rain forests and help prevent global warming. Another kid urged everyone to vote for Wilbur the Pig because he would bring about world peace, and if he didn't, then at least everyone would get a ham sandwich.

But Armpit knew he wasn't good at making jokes, and if

he didn't write his speech down, he would just stand there, sweating and babbling nervously. Besides, he really wanted Coo to win, for Ginny's sake.

X-Ray showed up a little before ten.

"Where are you off to?" Armpit's mother demanded.

"We just got to do something," Armpit said as he hurried outside, knowing he'd have to submit a sample when he returned.

It was the same H-E-B where his mother worked, although it had been a few years since she'd had to work the night shift. There were only a few cars in the parking lot, and no white Suburban.

"Man, I'm getting sick of getting jerked around by those jokers!" X-Ray complained.

"Just give 'em a couple of minutes," said Armpit. "He did say he lost his ATM card. Maybe he's having trouble getting the cash together."

"A couple a minutes," X-Ray agreed. "And then we're out of here. It's disrespect. What, they think we got nothing better to do than wait around for them? Disrespect."

Armpit was feeling claustrophobic in the car and stepped out to stretch.

"Good idea," said X-Ray. "Let 'em get a good look at you."

He looked up and down the aisles. "Maybe they're waiting at the other end of the parking lot," he suggested.

"I'm in the exact spot where I was earlier. The exact spot."

At a quarter after there was still no sign of them. "That's it," X-Ray announced. "We're leaving."

"Just wait a few more—" Armpit started, but X-Ray had already started the engine.

Armpit climbed back in, and they had only just started moving when a large white SUV pulled into the lot.

"Is that them?" Armpit asked.

X-Ray continued to drive away.

"Wait! It's a white Suburban."

"Too late!" X-Ray said as they bounced over a speed bump.

The horn sounded on the Suburban.

X-Ray yelled an obscenity out his window, then lurched out of the parking lot and into traffic.

"Are you nuts?" Armpit yelled. "That's two hundred and seventy dollars!"

"Our respect is worth a lot more than that," said X-Ray. "Who do they think they are?"

"If you don't sell the tickets, I'm going to kill you," Armpit warned him.

X-Ray laughed. "Always the joker."

9

Armpit felt pretty silly carrying Coo to school on Tuesday, and wished he had taken his backpack. He was still mad at X-Ray, but he was even madder at himself. The concert was four days away and no tickets had been sold. Six hundred and ninety dollars down the toilet.

"Hey, Armpit, want a ride?"

He glanced over to see a yellow Mustang slowly moving along beside him.

"Where you going, Armpit?"

There were five people in the car, three guys and two girls, and although he only recognized the two guys in the front seat, he knew he didn't want anything to do with any of them. The driver was named Donnell, and the guy beside him was Cole. Both were three or four years older than he was, and he was sort of surprised they knew his name. It was not good news.

"Come on, hop in," said Cole. "We'll take you where you want to go."

The trick was to say no without offending anyone, especially Cole, who was known to be a little bit crazy.

"It doesn't look like you got much room," Armpit said.

He wondered what they were doing out so early in the morning, then realized they must have been up all night. They were probably high.

"Always room for a brother. Sharese can sit on your lap."

"That's okay," said Armpit as he continued to walk. "I'm fine walking." He continued to walk and the car rolled slowly alongside him.

"What's the matter? You don't like Sharese?"

"Hi, Armpit," called a girl in the backseat.

"I just like to walk, that's all."

The car pulled ahead of him, and for a second he thought they were through with him, but then it swerved sharply into a driveway, blocking his path. The passenger door opened.

"You know, when a brother offers you a ride," said Cole, "the right thing to do is accept."

"I didn't mean any disrespect," Armpit said.

At least they all remained inside the car. He tried to act casual.

"What's with the bunny?" asked Sharese.

Armpit tightened his grip on Coo. "Something for school."

"School! It's summer!" shouted one of the guys from the back.

"It's so cute," Sharese said. "Can I have it?"

"It's for a school project."

"I want it," said Sharese.

Armpit tightened his grip on Coo. "It belongs to my neighbor." He'd fight all of them if he had to, before giving Coo up.

"That little white retard!" said Cole. "I seen you hangin' with her. Man, what's her problem?" He laughed.

Cole wasn't expecting an answer, but Armpit copied Ginny's tactic and gave him one.

"There was some bleeding inside her brain when she was born."

"Oh," Cole said. "Too bad."

Armpit slowly walked around the Mustang.

"What are you going to school for?" Cole shouted at him. "Come work with us, and you'll make all the money you'll ever need."

"Thanks, but it's just something I got to do."

He kept walking.

He heard the car door shut behind him but didn't turn around. A moment later he saw the car driving past him. Someone shouted "Fool!" out the window.

◆　◆　◆

Fifteen minutes later he stood in front of the class, all eyes on him, including Tatiana's.

"This is Coo," he began.

Everybody laughed.

"Coo has leukemia."

Some even laughed at that, too.

It wasn't that they were cruel. All the other speeches had been humorous and they expected more of the same. The sight of Armpit, the biggest and toughest kid in class, holding the little baby toy just added to the comedy, and it took a while for what he was saying to sink in.

He could feel his sweat dripping down his side and hoped it didn't show on his shirt.

"Coo belongs to my neighbor, Ginny. She has cerebral palsy."

"You just said she had leukemia," said Claire, Tatiana's friend.

"Coo has leukemia. Ginny has cerebral palsy. That's why Coo should be elected ruler of the world. Because Coo gives her comfort, courage, and confidence."

That was supposed to be his closing sentence. He didn't mean to say it so soon. He fumbled with his notecards, but he'd already gotten off wrong, so he just winged it.

"All her life, Ginny has had trouble walking and talking. Some kids at her school call her 'tard, you know, short for retard, but she's not retarded. She's really smart. It's just that her brain has difficulty processing information. It's like she has to decode everything first. That's why she stutters when she talks. She knows what she wants to say, but it's like her brain has trouble sending the signal to her mouth. And then if people pressure her, it just gets worse and worse, and she sometimes has these spastic seizures."

"And you want her to be ruler of the world?" somebody asked. Several people laughed.

"No, you should vote for Coo, Ginny's favorite stuffed animal. See, since I don't own any stuffed animals, Ginny gave me Coo. I told her I didn't want her favorite, you know, 'cause it's just for a stupid assignment."

The class erupted in laughter and Armpit realized that he probably shouldn't have called it a stupid assignment in front of Coach Simmons. He pressed on. "But Ginny said I had to take Coo. She said none of her others were as strong or as brave as Coo. Well, even though Ginny is only ten years old and has cerebral palsy and weighs less than sixty pounds, she's the strongest and bravest person I know. So if Coo could do that for Ginny, imagine what Coo could do for the world. So vote for Coo. Thanks."

He made his way back to his seat without looking at anyone. He had no idea if anything he'd said made any sense. At least it was over.

He was the first one out the door when the bell rang.

"Theodore," came a voice from behind him, and then Tatiana's hand was on his arm.

"I thought your speech was really sweet."

"Yeah, well, I didn't have any stuffed animals, so I had to borrow one."

She smiled her crooked smile. "You were really nervous, weren't you?"

"Sort of, yeah."

"I could tell. Don't worry. You did a really good job. I'm going to vote for Coo."

He smiled. "Thanks. I mean, it doesn't matter to me, but it would make Ginny really happy if Coo won."

"Can I see it?"

"Sure." He handed the stuffed animal to Tatiana.

"What exactly is a coo?"

Armpit laughed. "I don't know, some kind of bunny-person-thingy."

Tatiana hugged Coo. "It feels so soft. I like the way you said Coo will give you courage, comfort, and strength."

He didn't correct her.

"Armpit! Hey, Armpit!"

X-Ray came breezing down the hall. "Armpit! I thought I'd never find you."

He greeted Tatiana with a "hey," then pulled a wad of money out of his pocket and started counting it. "Twenty, forty, sixty, eighty, one hundred." He handed Armpit a hundred dollars but wasn't finished yet.

"Twenty, forty, sixty, eighty, two hundred."

He was still not finished.

"Twenty, forty, sixty . . ."

Tatiana was no longer smiling. "I better go," she said, handing Coo back to Armpit.

"Uh, see you later," Armpit said to her, but she didn't turn around as she quickly walked away.

X-Ray counted out another hundred dollars. In total, X-Ray gave him five hundred and thirty dollars.

Armpit could hardly believe it. He had gotten practically all his money back. It was money he'd thought he'd never see again. "Was it the guys in the Suburban?"

"Those clowns? Hell no! A lady called me this morning. Wanted four tickets for her kid's birthday. The whole thing took twenty minutes. See, that's the way you do business. Not some jokers stringing you along like you're a yo-yo."

Armpit felt bad for having doubted X-Ray. "Wait a second," he said. "Four tickets should be five hundred and *forty*."

"Oh, yeah, I needed to borrow ten. You don't mind, do you?"

10

It's a six-and-a-half-hour bus ride from Baton Rouge to Houston along I-10. Six buses and two trucks were making the journey. Kaira DeLeon's bus was equipped with a flat-screen TV, a DVD player, two video game players, a refrigerator, a microwave, a treadmill, and a bathroom that included a shower as well as a makeup area. The only person on that bus, however, was the bus driver.

Kaira was sick of being alone and so had asked the guys in the band if she could ride with them. It was her first time on their bus and she knew her mother would freak if she found out. Her mother imagined all kinds of wild goings-on with a rock 'n' roll band, but all they were doing was playing cards. Tim B, the lead guitarist, had given her a beer, but she didn't like the taste and only took a few sips to be polite.

"Which way do we pass this time?" asked Duncan, a bald man with a goatee. He wore dark sunglasses, indoors or out. As far as Kaira could tell, all bass players always wore sunglasses.

"Left," said Cotton, the drummer, who then handed three cards to Kaira. Cotton was also bald, but that was because he shaved his head. Duncan still had hair on the sides.

"We passed left last time," said Billy Goat, whose last name was really Gotleib. He played keyboard.

"Too late, I already picked up my cards," said Cotton.

They may have been wild rock 'n' rollers at one time in their lives, but to Kaira they just seemed like a bunch of old men.

The Grateful Dead was playing over the sound system. She found the music monotonous but didn't dare say so out loud. That would have been sacrilege to these guys. She also pretended their cigarette smoke didn't bother her. Anything was better than another long ride alone.

She knew they all thought she was just a spoiled prima donna who didn't know anything about music. She'd heard them say as much. They'd been making music long before she was born, and often mentioned names of famous people they'd played with, names she'd never heard.

"Okay, who's got the two of clubs?" Kaira asked. "Oh, I do." She giggled, then placed the card on the coffee table.

She had never played hearts with real people before, only on a computer, and was losing badly. It seemed like every hand she got stuck with the queen of spades.

The bus had two couches set up at a right angle, with a

coffee table in the center "for drinks and feet." Those were Cotton's words. Just about everything he said made her laugh.

Three other band members and all three backup singers had missed the bus. They would have to find their own way to Houston.

"Goin' to Texas, we should listen to some Texas music," said Tim B. He stood up, then stumbled and fell against the side of the couch. Kaira didn't know if this was caused by the bus's movement or by what he'd been drinking.

"I'm all right," he said, getting back to his feet, then made his way to the CD rack. "Hey, Kaira, you ever heard of Janis Joplin?"

Kaira hesitated a moment, then said, "Oh, yeah, she really rocks!"

Cotton saw right through her. "You never heard of her, have you?"

"Uh, maybe, I'm not sure."

"If you heard her, you'd know," he said.

"We're talking real music," Tim B said as he fumbled with the CD. "Raw and to the bone."

"And no cutesy-dootsy backup singers," said Duncan.

"I'll drink to that," said Cotton, clinking beer bottles with him.

Kaira didn't like the backup singers any better than they did, but El Genius said they added sexual energy.

"Music needs blank spaces sometimes," Cotton said. "They take up all the blank spaces."

"Now you're talkin' about music," said Billy Goat. "Nobody makes real music anymore. It's all just a big show."

"Just background for MTV," said Duncan. "It's almost impossible for a real musician to do anything worth listening to anymore. Now it's all I-don't-know-what."

"Don't listen to them, Kaira," said Cotton. "They been saying the same thing for the last twenty-five years."

Janis Joplin's voice came over the speakers. Kaira hadn't heard her before, but she liked her right off. Her raspy voice seemed to drip emotion. There was a kind of raw energy to the music, not like the polished songs she sang, in which every note was carefully planned and orchestrated.

"Now, that's the way rock 'n' roll's supposed to be," said Tim B, half sitting down, half falling onto the couch.

"She's from Port Arthur, Texas," said Cotton.

"Where's that?"

None of the band members seemed to know.

"Somewhere in Texas," said Cotton.

Kaira laughed.

"So, Kaira," said Billy Goat. "I thought your mama didn't allow you to ride with us."

"She doesn't know I'm here," said Kaira. "Anyway, I got Fred to protect me from you dirty old men."

The Doofus was sitting up front next to the driver.

"Yeah, well, tell you what," said Billy Goat. "Your mama would be a lot better off if she kept her watchful eye on that husband of hers instead of on you."

"Don't go there," said Cotton.

"What do you mean by that?" asked Kaira.

"*Her watchful eye . . .* ," sang Tim B.

"It's nothing," said Cotton.

"She's a grown girl," said Billy. "She might as well know the truth."

"You don't even know what you're talking about," said Cotton.

"What?" asked Kaira.

"All I'm saying," said Billy, "is your mama would be better off if she kept one eye on her husband and one eye on Aileen."

"And all I'm saying," said Cotton, "is when you don't know what you're talking about, you shouldn't talk so much."

"Aileen's my mom's friend," said Kaira. "They go shopping together."

"She's your dad's friend too," Tim B said with a laugh.

"He's not my dad," said Kaira.

"The girl likes to shop, I'll give you that," said Duncan. "But the question is this: whose money is she spending?"

Aileen was the person in charge of coordinating all the travel arrangements for the tour. She had been the one who went and got Pillow when Kaira had left it behind in Connecticut. Kaira's father had given Pillow to her when she was three years old. When Aileen had called the hotel, the manager said they hadn't found any extra pillows, but Aileen didn't take no for an answer. She took a flight back to Connecticut, went to the hotel, and personally searched the laundry room until she found it.

Kaira didn't know what to think now. Aileen just seemed to be someone who really had her act together. So besides the fact that Aileen would be betraying Kaira's mother, Kaira just couldn't imagine someone as smart and as cool as her being involved with someone as gross as El Genius.

Before Aileen started going along with Kaira's mother on her shopping sprees, Kaira's mother usually came home looking all gaudy and ridiculous. When Aileen went with her, the stuff she bought actually looked pretty good on her.

Aileen had good taste. At least in *clothes*.

Well, if El Genius really was cheating on her mother, then maybe that wasn't all bad, Kaira decided. Maybe her mom would divorce the freak!

She listened to Janis sing the blues, her voice filled with suffering, yet tenderness.

"Maybe we can meet Janis while we're in Texas?" she said.

Duncan and Tim B laughed.

"We'll all be meeting Janis someday," said Cotton. "But it won't be in Texas."

Janis had died of a drug overdose over forty years ago. She was only twenty-seven at the time.

"Hey, Kaira, ever hear of the Beatles?" asked Duncan.

"Who?" asked Kaira.

"You got to be kiddin' me," said Duncan. "You're kidding me, right?"

Kaira shrugged.

Cotton laughed. "She's playing with you, man."

Duncan wasn't so sure.

When they arrived at the hotel in Houston, Aileen was there to give them all their room keys and schedules. She had arrived earlier and had already gotten everybody checked in. They could just go right to their rooms. Their luggage would be brought up.

"You're Rhoda Morgenstern," she told Kaira as she handed her the key.

Kaira studied Aileen's face for some hint of betrayal, but her expression gave nothing away.

Even in her high heels, Aileen was shorter than Kaira. Everything about her was small: her waist, her feet, her ears, her mouth. She was stylish, efficient, and compact, like a cell phone.

"Do you know who Rhoda is?" Aileen asked.

"Mary Tyler Moore's best friend," said Kaira.

"Actually, Mary Richards's best friend," said Aileen.

It was a game they had. Aileen always registered Kaira under an assumed name so she wouldn't be hassled by fans. Aileen chose characters from old TV shows, but Kaira hadn't been stumped yet.

She watched too much TV.

11

X-Ray picked up Armpit at school; then they drove to South Congress Avenue in search of a barbecue joint called Smokestack Lightnin'. Somebody by the name of Murdock wanted two tickets.

"I don't feel comfortable on someone else's territory," X-Ray had said.

"How come he couldn't meet you at the H-E-B?"

"Said he couldn't get away. Works from six in the morning until midnight."

Armpit thought that sounded a little suspicious.

So did X-Ray. That was why he wanted Armpit along.

"I got to be at work at one," Armpit reminded him.

"I'll get you there," X-Ray assured him.

Congress Avenue was called that because at its north

74

end stood the majestic state capitol building, with its dome and white columns. This was where the Texas congress met, but only every other year, so they couldn't cause too much damage.

Just south of the capitol was the financial and theater district, and then the Congress Street Bridge, which crossed over Town Lake. A colony of more than a million Mexican free-tailed bats lived in the cracks and crevices on the underside of the bridge. Several fancy hotels lined the banks of the lake—which actually was not a lake at all but a river—and tourists would gather at sundown to watch the bats swarm out from under the bridge as they went in search of food.

They kept the mosquito population under control.

"Is Murdock his first name or his last?" Armpit asked as they drove across the bridge.

A girl wearing very short pants and a bikini top was jogging with her dog.

"Whoo! Whoo!" X-Ray shouted through Armpit's open window.

The girl raised her middle finger.

South Congress Avenue hardly resembled the street north of the river. Armpit looked out at boarded-up buildings, liquor stores, bars, and tattoo parlors. At night the area would come alive with some of the best music in Austin, but in the heat and glare of the late-morning sun, it seemed as if the entire street suffered from a giant hangover.

"There it is," said X-Ray.

SMOKESTACK LIGHTNIN was painted in brown letters on

the smoky glass of a storefront restaurant located next to the Fingernail Emporium. Armpit could smell the slow-cooked meat as soon as he stepped out of the car. If they hadn't been there to sell tickets, he wouldn't have minded a sausage wrap or a chopped-beef sandwich. He had missed lunch, thanks to X-Ray.

"Here, you better hold these," X-Ray said, handing Armpit the tickets.

He hadn't seen them since the day they bought them. Once again, he noticed *This ticket may not be resold* clearly printed on the back.

A bell on the door jangled as X-Ray pushed it open. Armpit followed him inside.

Only a couple of tables were occupied, but it wasn't noon yet. A roll of brown paper towels stood in the center of every table, along with various bottles of hot sauce.

They made their way to the front.

"What can I get you?" asked the man behind the counter. Various meats were on display behind a dirty glass window.

"We're looking for Murdock," said X-Ray.

"You found him."

He was a black man with gray hair and a gray beard. His apron was splattered with grease and barbecue sauce.

"X-Ray?"

"Yeah, and this is my partner, Armpit."

Murdock laughed at the name. "Armpit, huh? I used to know a dude who called himself Burnt Toast. He played the slide trombone. You play an instrument, Armpit?"

Armpit wanted to tell him about the scorpion but instead just shook his head.

"Let me see the tickets?"

Armpit felt a little worried as he handed the tickets over the glass case. There wasn't a whole lot they could do if Murdock decided just to keep them.

Murdock looked them over. "Row M. Not bad. Two hundred and seventy, right?"

"That's right," said X-Ray. "And you're getting a bargain."

"Well, I don't know about that," said Murdock. "But I only get to see my daughter one weekend a month, so I gotta make the most of it. When she heard Kaira DeLeon was going to be playing, it was all she could talk about. Hey, Wiley, you ever listen to Kaira DeLeon?"

"Who?" asked one of the few customers in the place.

"Kaira DeLeon."

"Never heard a her."

Wiley wore a Harley T-shirt and had tattoos up and down both arms.

"Go punch E-4," Murdock told him. "See if she don't knock your socks off." He turned his attention back to X-Ray. "I really do appreciate you boys coming all the way down here. When it's your own business, you got to stay on top of it twenty-four hours a day. I do it all: cook, wash dishes, you name it."

Armpit was still waiting for either the money or Murdock to return the tickets.

Wiley fumbled with the jukebox. He was a big guy, and

Armpit would not want to have to try to deal with him and Murdock.

"Can I get you something to eat?" Murdock asked. "On the house."

"Chopped-beef sandwich," X-Ray answered right away.

"How 'bout you, Armpit?"

He was more concerned about the money than he was about food. "The same," he said.

"You like your sauce hot or mild?" Murdock asked.

"Mild," said X-Ray.

"Armpit?"

"The same."

Kaira's voice filled the restaurant.

> *I'm not the kinda girl who's apt to . . .*
> *Settle down.*
> *No, I'm the kinda girl who likes to . . .*
> *Get around.*

Murdock brought the sandwiches over to the cash register. He opened it, then took out two hundred and seventy dollars, which he gave to X-Ray, along with his sandwich.

Armpit felt bad about not trusting him.

> *I see you lookin' at me*
> *the way you do . . .*
> *Just hold on!*
> *a little longer.*

Just hold on!
a little bit longer.
Hold on, baby
just a little bit longer
'Cause I'll get around to you!

Murdock laughed. "Man, don't you just love her?"

"She's all right," said Wiley.

"So what do you want to drink?" Murdock asked X-Ray.

Next to the cash register was a large metal bucket filled with ice and soft drinks.

"Root beer," said X-Ray.

Murdock looked at Armpit. "Let me guess. The same?"

Armpit shrugged.

"Does he tell you when to go to the bathroom, too?"

Armpit smiled and sheepishly shrugged.

And now that you got me . . .
in your arms,
Ooh, I feel so . . .
soft and warm.
There's only one thing
I want to say . . .

Armpit bit into his sandwich. He'd eaten a lot of barbecue in his life, but this might have been the very best. Of course, that might have had something to do with the fact that he now had all his money back, and then some.

Just hold on!
a little longer.
Just hold on!
a little bit longer.
Hold on, baby,
just a little bit longer
And then I'll be on my way.

12

X-Ray sold four more tickets to a couple of high school students from Westlake, and just like that, Armpit had another two hundred and seventy dollars. He was up three hundred dollars, and there were still two tickets left, which would mean another hundred and thirty-five for him.

The final two ruler-of-the-world campaign speeches were given Thursday morning. The second-to-last speech was given by Claire, Tatiana's friend, who brought Dumbo the Elephant.

". . . so all the other elephants made fun of him, but then he got drunk and ended up in a tree, and these birds sang to him. And then his mouse friend said he could fly because of a magic feather. . . ."

"Yeah, I've seen the movie," a boy in back said, but Claire just continued.

"I used to love that movie!" Armpit heard Tatiana whisper. He wondered if she still planned to vote for Coo.

The last speech, given by Robbie Kinkaid, was for an armadillo name Joe. Robbie obviously made up the speech as he went along, including the name of his armadillo.

"This is an armadillo, I think. You can vote for him if you want. His name is . . . Joe. Joe the Armadillo. He's brown, and has four legs, and this shell thingy. . . ."

Then came the vote.

Everyone had to write down his or her first and second choices.

Joe the Armadillo won, and Dumbo was elected vice ruler of the world. If for any reason Joe was unable to fulfill his obligations, Dumbo would take over.

Armpit tried not to let his disappointment show. After all, it was just a stupid assignment, and people just voted for the only ones they could remember.

"I'm sorry Coo didn't win," Tatiana said to him after class. She placed her hand on his arm as she said it.

"No biggie."

"You gave the best speech," she told him, her hand still there.

"It would have made Ginny happy."

"She's your sister?"

"My neighbor."

"That's right. She has leukemia?"

"Cerebral palsy."

Armpit wondered if Tatiana had forgotten her hand was there, but if she had, he wasn't about to remind her. Her fingernails were painted green. Her perfume smelled like cantaloupe.

"Say, listen," he said. "Do you like Kaira DeLeon?"

She squeezed his arm. " 'Red Alert!' I love that song."

"You want to go to the concert on Saturday?"

She bit her lip. "You mean with you?"

"Yeah."

"Yeah."

"Yeah?" he asked, just to make sure.

She smiled. "Yeah."

By the time economics was over, Armpit had convinced himself that X-Ray had already sold the last two tickets and that he was going to have to buy two from a scalper for fifteen hundred dollars. He could hear X-Ray's voice in his head. "Seven hundred and fifty dollars—*each*."

When the bell rang he bolted out of his seat and hurried to the office, where he asked the secretary if he could use the phone. She seemed sympathetic, but it was against school policy. Apparently not the principal, the superintendent, or even the president of the United States could change school policy.

Where was Joe the Armadillo when you needed him?

He left the office and spotted Matt Kapok, a skinny white guy from his economics class. Matt was probably the only student in his class who was taking summer school because he *wanted* to, not because he had to.

"Matt!" Armpit shouted as he charged toward him. "You got fifty cents? I'm desperate, man!"

Matt backed up against a row of lockers as he took his wallet out of his back pocket. "Uh, sure. Here." He held out a dollar, but it dropped out of his hand before Armpit could take it.

As Armpit bent down to pick it up, Matt sidestepped him and quickly disappeared around the corner.

"I'll pay you back!" Armpit called after him, but didn't know if Matt heard him.

He went back to the office, where the secretary gave him four quarters for the dollar, then went to the pay phone and called X-Ray.

"You sell the last two tickets?"

"Not to worry, not to worry," X-Ray said in a soothing voice.

"Have you sold them!"

"Look, you got to—"

"Yes or no?"

"Not yet, but—"

"Don't!"

"Wait a second. Who are you, and what have you done with Armpit?"

Armpit told him about Tatiana. "She had her hand on my arm, and with her perfume and everything, I couldn't think straight."

"Was she the one I saw you talkin' to that time? Strange hair, goofy smile?"

"Yeah."

"She's pretty cute."

"I'll pay you a hundred and thirty-five for the two tickets," said Armpit. "That woulda been your share if you sold them."

A hundred and thirty-five seemed like a bargain. He was relieved not to have to pay fifteen hundred.

"Man, that girl's really gotten to you," said X-Ray. "Look, they're your tickets. You don't have to buy them twice!" He laughed. "That musta been some perfume!"

13

"Well, that's the way it goes," Ginny said when Armpit told her that Coo didn't win. They were taking their daily walk around the block.

"What they should have done," said Armpit, "is write down all the candidates' names on a ballot. The problem was nobody remembered any of the speeches."

"Well, that's the way it goes," Ginny said again.

Her face twitched as she said it, and Armpit didn't know if that was due to her disability or if she was trying not to cry.

"But hey, I got an A on my speech," he said. "Thanks to Coo." He smiled. "Of course, it doesn't hurt that Coach Simmons thinks I'll be going out for football."

"Like how Mrs. R-Randsinkle g-gave m-me an A in art," said Ginny.

Mrs. Randsinkle had been her teacher last year.

"And I c-c-couldn't even c-c-color inside the l-lines."

Armpit noticed that Ginny stuttered more when she talked about school.

"Well, you know, art's not just about coloring in the lines," said Armpit. "It's about creativity. Putting your soul on the paper. You're good at that."

"No, she just felt sorry for me. She w-w-wished I w-wasn't in her class. She's afraid of my s-seizures."

Armpit would have liked to tell her that wasn't true, but he knew it probably was. Ginny had enough problems without him telling her she was wrong. "Well, they are kind of scary," he said. "But I bet there's a lot she liked about you too. You're a very thoughtful and caring person."

Ginny's arm was raised, but this time she noticed it herself and lowered it.

"Oh, I didn't tell you! I asked a girl to go to the Kaira DeLeon concert with me."

Ginny covered her gaping mouth with her hand. From behind it, she asked, "What'd she say?"

"She said yeah."

Ginny giggled.

"What's so funny?"

"The w-way y-you l-look."

"How do I look?"

"All dreamy-eyed." She giggled some more. "What's her name?" she asked in a teasing kind of voice.

"Tatiana."

Ginny giggled.

"What?"

"The way you said it."

"How did I say it?"

"Tati-*ahna.*"

"Tatiana," said Armpit, trying to sound normal.

"Tati-*ahna,*" said Ginny. "Is she pretty?"

"Yeah, but in a different kind of way. It's like that Kaira DeLeon song 'Imperfection'? You know?" He sang: *"You reflect on your reflection. But you will never see. Your imperfection is your finest quality."*

Ginny laughed. He wasn't a very good singer.

"She's cute because of all her imperfections," Armpit explained.

"I knew it!" said Ginny. "I smelled her p-perfume on Coo."

Armpit remembered Tatiana had hugged Coo.

"Tati-*ahna,*" teased Ginny.

"I don't even know if she really likes me," Armpit said. "I think she's just a big Kaira DeLeon fan."

"She likes you," said Ginny.

"Oh, yeah? How do you know?"

"Because. You're a v-very thoughtful and caring p-person."

While Ginny and Armpit were walking around the block, Tatiana was sitting on the floor of Claire's bedroom, along with their friend Roxanne. They were sharing a bowl of popcorn and drinking diet sodas.

"Aren't you just a little bit scared?" Roxanne asked.

"No, why should I be?"

Claire and Roxanne looked at each other knowingly.

"He is kind of dangerous," said Claire.

"Maybe that's what she likes about him," said Roxanne. "The *danger!*"

"He's a nice guy," said Tatiana. "He's sweet."

"Sweet? He almost *killed* two people, girl!" Roxanne reminded her.

"Do you know what they called him at Camp Green Lake?" asked Claire.

"Yes, I know," said Tatiana.

"Armpit!" Claire said. "Out of all those nasty, sweaty guys, he smelled the worst!"

"It was so bad, even the other sweaty guys noticed," said Roxanne. "And you know *guys!* It's gotta stink really bad before they notice."

"And you really want to sit next to him, in that hot arena, with everyone all jammed close together?" asked Claire.

"He'll probably put his big, fat, sweaty arm around you," said Roxanne.

"I like 'Red Alert!' " said Tatiana. "I think it'll be cool to see Kaira DeLeon sing it in person."

Armpit stopped in the restroom before school on Friday and splashed his face with cold water. Then he caught up with Tatiana just before she got to class.

"My friend said I could use his car. One of the doors doesn't open, but at least I got wheels."

"That's great," said Tatiana without looking at him. She entered the classroom and maneuvered her way between the desks. Claire whispered something to her when she sat down, and Tatiana said something back.

Armpit couldn't hear what they said, but he was able to read Tatiana's lips. She told Claire to shut up.

He went to work early on Saturday, glad to be doing physical labor so he wouldn't drive himself crazy thinking about the concert and Tatiana. Hernandez dumped a truckload of dirt in the driveway, and now they mixed it with peat moss before spreading it around the yard.

Better to use a fifty-cent plant and ten-dollar dirt than a ten-dollar plant and fifty-cent dirt. Jack Dunlevy said that all the time.

He got home around four-thirty but didn't shower right away, or else he'd be all sweaty again by the time he picked up Tatiana. Instead, he went over to Ginny's.

Ginny's mother looked all frazzled when she opened the door. "Oh, Theodore, I'm so glad you're here," she said. "Ginny's— It's my fault. I said something I shouldn't have."

Armpit stepped inside. "Ginny, are you okay?"

She sat on the floor, crying while she hugged Coo.

"Ginny, what's wrong?"

"My d-d-dad . . ." She was unable to continue.

"Did your dad call?"

Her father had left home when she was a baby.

"He l-left because of m-me. B-because of my disa-b-b-bility."

"That's not what I said!" said her mother.

"It's true!" Ginny exclaimed.

"It wasn't you. It was the whole situation."

"If I g-get b-b-better, will he c-come h-h-home?"

Ginny's mom was crying now too.

Armpit sat on the floor next to Ginny. "I didn't know your dad was disabled," he said.

"He's n-not."

"Sounds like he is. He's a lot worse off than you are. You just had a little bleeding in your brain. He's got something wrong with his soul. I mean, if he left your mom and you, man, there's got to be something really wrong with him."

Ginny shrugged.

"I sure hope he gets better. You at least can go to physical therapy. I don't know what they can do for someone with no heart and soul."

There was a knock on the door; then it opened, and Armpit's mother leaned her head in. "Is Theodore here?" She had the telephone with her, her hand covering the mouthpiece. "It's *her*."

His mother was almost as excited about his date as he was, even though he kept telling her it wasn't a *date*. They were just going to hang out at the concert together.

He took the phone and walked outside for privacy. "Hello?"

"Hi, how's it goin'?" asked Tatiana.

"Great. I'm really looking forward to the concert."

"Look, I don't know how to say it. I'm not good at this."

"At what?"

"I'm really sorry, but I can't go to the concert."

He didn't respond.

"Theodore? You there?"

"Yeah."

"I'm really sorry. There's this family thing I got to do. I forgot all about it. They won't let me out of it. My parents have this thing about *family time!*"

"I understand," said Armpit.

"You sure?"

"Yeah."

"But I want you to tell me all about it on Monday, okay?"

"Sure."

"Promise? Every song she sings. What clothes she's wearing. I want to know *everything!*"

"Okay."

"I really feel bad about this. Maybe you can find someone else to go with you."

"Yeah, don't worry about it."

He hung up, then dialed X-Ray's number.

"Was it Tati-*ahna?*" Ginny teased when he returned to her house. She seemed to be feeling better.

"She can't go to the concert."

"Oh, I'm so sorry," her mother said.

"Well, that's the way it goes," Armpit said. He winked at Ginny.

"You want to hold Coo?" she offered.

He shook his head. X-Ray had said people were still calling about the tickets, so maybe it wasn't too late. If nothing else, they could go to the Lonestar and try to sell them at the door.

But now another thought came to him. "So, Ginny," he said. "You want to go to the concert with me?"

Her eyes widened. She looked to her mother, who shrugged, then nodded her approval.

14

"Just don't come home with your nose pierced," Ginny's mother told her.

Ginny promised she wouldn't.

Armpit's parents seemed more worried about Ginny's safety than her own mother, but Armpit had a lot to do with that since his natural response was to argue with anything they said.

"Now, you keep a sharp eye on Ginny at all times."

"She can take care of herself."

"There are a lot of crazy people at a rock concert."

"Just because people have tattoos or pierced tongues doesn't mean they're crazy!"

"If you're not going to be responsible . . ."

"Ginny's mother trusts me. Why can't my own parents?"

"Because we know you."

He didn't know why he argued with them like that. He was just as concerned as they were, if not more so. He knew a rock concert could be a wild scene and had every intention of protecting Ginny and holding her hand until they were safely in their seats.

He called X-Ray to make sure he hadn't already sold the tickets.

"I got a guy on the line right now!" X-Ray said. "He said he'd pay a hundred and fifty a ticket. I told you the price would only go up. Didn't I tell you?"

"You can't sell them. I'm taking Ginny."

"Ginny? Are you outta your gourd? Have you completely lost your mind?"

"Look, she had a really bad day. Just bring the tickets over here. I want to get an early start so we can beat the crowds."

"We're talking three hundred dollars!"

"I promised Ginny."

X-Ray said he'd be over in twenty minutes, but he did not sound happy about it.

Armpit sighed as he set the phone back in its cradle. Maybe he was crazy. He didn't even know if Ginny would be able to handle the loud music and the crowds.

The phone rang a moment later. It was X-Ray again.

"I told the guy they were no longer for sale, and he offered two hundred a ticket."

"No," said Armpit.

"Four hundred dollars!"

"No."

It was almost seven o'clock. X-Ray still hadn't showed. Armpit and Ginny waited on the front porch, along with Ginny's mother.

"You listen to Theodore and do everything he tells you," said her mother.

"I will," Ginny promised.

He would be driving Ginny's mother's car. She insisted on it, which was fine with him, because if he took the X-Mobile they'd have to first take X-Ray home and they were running out of time. Besides, Ginny's mother's Camry was undoubtedly more reliable, and safer, than X-Ray's machine.

His mother came outside. "Still not here?"

Armpit shook his head.

"You must be very proud of Theodore," said Ginny's mother.

Armpit's mother was caught off guard. "Uh, well, yes, of course I am."

If he sold those tickets I'm going to kill him, Armpit thought, and then a second later the X-Mobile pulled around the corner.

X-Ray parked in front and slid out the passenger side as Armpit and Ginny headed down to meet him.

"What took you so long?" Armpit demanded.

X-Ray ignored the question. "Hey, Ginny, are you ready to *rock 'n' roll?*"

96

"Yes."

X-Ray laughed, then handed Armpit the envelope containing the two remaining tickets. "Just remember," he said. "Be flexible."

"All right," said Armpit.

"You hear what I'm saying? *Flexible*."

"Yeah, I hear you," Armpit said. He didn't have time for any of X-Ray's nonsense.

He and Ginny got into her mother's car; then he carefully backed it out of the driveway while everyone waved good-bye. He saw X-Ray say something to Ginny's mother, who laughed.

They turned the corner. The clock on the dashboard read 7:06. The concert wasn't until eight.

He winked at Ginny. She shut and opened both eyes.

Armpit sang: *"I'm gonna take you for a ride! And we're gonna have some fun! I'm gonna take you for a ride!"*

Ginny joined in: *"And we're gonna have some fun!"*

Armpit: *"I'm gonna take you someplace you never been before . . ."*

They sang the last line together. *"And you'll never be the same again!"*

15

They sang all the way to the Lonestar Arena. "You know, you don't stutter at all when you sing," Armpit pointed out.

Ginny laughed.

"Maybe you should sing all the time."

Ginny laughed again. "*Good mor-ning,*" she sang. "*I'll have pan-cakes.*"

Armpit laughed as he pulled into the parking lot, which was crammed with cars and people.

Ginny sang, "*Two plus two is four, Mrs. Randsinkle.*"

He couldn't find anything that resembled a parking space. It was X-Ray's fault for being so late.

He lifted the handicapped placard out of the pocket in the door beside him. "I'm going to have to use this," he said.

Ginny stopped singing.

"It's not because I don't think you can walk."

Ginny nodded. "I know," she said.

He hung the placard on the rearview mirror and parked right in front.

Ginny tightly held Armpit's hand as they made their way to the building. She was so excited she would have fallen several times if he hadn't been holding her up. "Small steps," he reminded her.

"Is she all right?" the ticket taker asked.

"She's dancing," Armpit told him.

Inside, they had to maneuver their way through throngs of people all moving in different directions. Before going to their seats, they got in a long line at one of the concession counters. Ginny's mother had given her twenty dollars.

Armpit lifted Ginny up on his shoulders so she could see. She really wanted to get a Kaira DeLeon official tour T-shirt, but when they got to the front, they were told it cost twenty-eight dollars.

Armpit was willing to pay the other eight dollars, plus tax, but Ginny's mother had told her not to let Theodore pay for anything. Instead, Ginny bought two soft drinks, which came in plastic souvenir cups, and a bucket of popcorn for them to share. She paid with her twenty-dollar bill and got one dollar and seventy-five cents back in change.

Armpit held the popcorn and his drink, while Ginny held on to her drink and his arm, as they slowly made their way to their seats. He couldn't help thinking about the last time he'd held a bucket of popcorn in a crowded place, but they safely reached section B, row M, seats 1 and 2 without incident.

The large stage, with giant towers of speakers on either side, jutted out in front of them. Behind them were at least forty rows of seats, and those were the good seats. Beyond those, and to the sides, were two tiers of bleachers.

He glanced around at the people seated nearby, realizing they were the ones to whom X-Ray sold the tickets. Well, at least they got their money's worth. These really were great seats.

"Great seats, huh?" he said.

"Yes," said Ginny.

He looked for Murdock but didn't see him. An African American girl was sitting a few seats away with her boyfriend. If she was Murdock's daughter, then that was too bad. He remembered Murdock had bought the tickets so he could spend time with his daughter on the one weekend a month he got to see her.

Backstage, Kaira DeLeon was chewing a piece of gum that had long lost its flavor. This was always the worst time for her. She knew she'd be all right once she started singing. Then she would disappear into the music.

The backstage area was filled with people, half of whom she didn't recognize. Besides all the people working on tour, there were record company executives, friends of record company executives, children of lawyers, brothers-in-law of security personnel. Every once in a while someone managed to slip past the Doofus and ask for her autograph. In Houston, a woman and her two kids had actually asked her to sing a song for them.

Kaira wore a lavender sweat suit. Beneath it was the outfit she'd wear for the show, which was little more than sparkling underwear with fringe. For some reason it seemed all right to dress that way in front of thousands of people, but in this small area it would have been embarrassing.

She wished she had stayed in her dressing room instead of having to be around all these people. It was almost eight, but the concerts never started on time. She should know that by now. El Genius liked to "make 'em wait." He didn't want her taking the stage until the audience had worked itself into a frenzy.

She looked at him, shouting into his walkie-talkie. She pitied the person on the other end. Next to him, her mother was drinking from one of those horrible plastic souvenir cups with her picture on it. Lately her mother had begun having cocktails during the show.

At least Aileen wasn't around. Kaira could no longer stand the sight of her. She'd already gone to Dallas to make sure all the arrangements had been taken care of at their next hotel.

Kaira wondered if her mother suspected there was something going on between Jerome and Aileen. Maybe that was the reason for the cocktails.

A local DJ was onstage now, firing up the crowd.

"Is everyone ready?"

◆ ◆ ◆

"Yes!" Ginny shouted at the top of her lungs, but even Armpit, sitting right next to her, couldn't hear her for the crowd.

"Are you sure?"

"Yes!" he and Ginny shouted.

"Because Kaira DeLeon will be standing on this very spot in just five minutes!"

Armpit felt Ginny's fingernails dig into his arm.

"So just hold on a little longer!"

Everyone cheered the line from one of Kaira's songs.

Armpit only slowly became aware that somebody was tapping his shoulder. He turned to see a security guard.

"Excuse me," the guard said, apparently not for the first time. "May I see your tickets, please?"

A man and young girl stood behind him. The girl was probably Ginny's age, although she was much bigger.

"May I see your tickets, please?" the security guard asked again.

"My tickets?"

"Please."

Armpit tried to remember what he'd done with them. He hoped he hadn't dropped them when he was dealing with the popcorn and soda.

"You're sitting in our seats!" the girl accused.

"Are n-n-not!" said Ginny.

Armpit stood up to check his pockets. The security guard instinctively stepped back from him.

"I don't want any trouble," the guard said, placing a hand on his walkie-talkie. "I just want to make sure you're in your right seats."

Armpit didn't want any trouble either. "I got them here somewhere."

"I'm going to have to ask you to come with me, Sir."

"I've got the tickets!" Armpit shouted, partly out of frustration and partly to be heard over the crowd, which was now stomping their feet with impatience.

"Please come with me, sir, and I'll help you find your correct seats."

"Just wait!"

The guard spoke into his walkie-talkie. "I'm going to need some help here. Section B."

Armpit's pants had too many pockets: three on the right front, two on the left front, and two in the back. "Found 'em!" he exclaimed. They were in one of the front pockets. He handed the stubs to the security guard.

As the guard was looking them over, two uniformed police officers hurried quickly down the aisle. "What's the problem here?" asked one of the officers.

"No problem," said Armpit.

"Counterfeit tickets," said the security guard. "He refuses to leave."

"What?" Armpit exclaimed, reaching for the tickets. "Let me see . . ."

An officer grabbed his arm and twisted it behind his back, spinning him around.

Armpit jerked himself free, but the other officer grabbed him.

The next thing he knew he was on the floor, his face pressed against the concrete. He could feel a knee digging into the small of his back.

It felt like his arms were being ripped out of their sockets as first one, then the other was jerked behind his back. Then they were handcuffed together.

His head was lifted off the floor by his hair and a police officer shouted in his face. "What's she on?"

"What'd you give her?" shouted the other officer.

He winced in pain. It felt like his hair was about to be ripped right out of his head. He could hear the security guard calling for a doctor. "We're going to have to pump her stomach!"

The officer abruptly let go of his hair, and his face banged against the floor. "Look," the officer said, no longer shouting. "It would really help for us to know what kind of drugs we're dealing with here."

"You think it's bad now," said the other one. "Believe me, you do not want anything to happen to her."

"Help us save her life!"

"What's she on!"

Armpit managed to get a glimpse of Ginny, her body jerking around uncontrollably on the floor.

The sight of her made him lurch up, knocking both officers backward, but just for a moment. They quickly tackled

104

him again, and then a billy club slammed against the side of his neck.

"What's going on here?"

It was a woman's voice.

"Stay back, Mayor, he's all whacked out on something."

"You don't hit somebody who's already on the ground, in handcuffs," said Cherry Lane.

"He drugged that little girl."

"She's not on drugs!" Armpit gasped.

"Shut up!" said the officer, pushing his head against the floor.

He managed to raise his face back up. "I dug a trench at your house!" he gasped. "You said you admired me!"

The mayor leaned down with her hands on her knees to get a better look at him. Her long silver hair hung on both sides of her face. "You work for Jack Dunlevy?"

"Yes!"

"What's wrong with the girl?"

"She's not on drugs. I swear. She's having a seizure."

"He was caught with counterfeit tickets," said one of the officers.

"Let me help her," Armpit pleaded. "Please."

"You think *he knew* they were counterfeit?" asked the mayor. "You think he'd sit in those seats if he knew they were counterfeit?"

"I can help her," said Armpit.

"Let him go!" ordered the mayor.

"I don't think that's a good idea."

"You let him go right now, unless you want to spend the next ten years walking up and down Lamar Boulevard."

The officer twisted Armpit's arm extra hard as he unlocked the handcuffs. The other officer was ready with his baton.

Staying low, Armpit hurried to Ginny. Drool dripped from her mouth as her body writhed and twitched. Her eyes were wide open, but they weren't seeing anything.

The floor was sticky with spilled drinks and popcorn.

"I'm here now, Ginny," he said softly. "I'm here now." He wiped the drool off her face and adjusted her glasses, which had fallen to one side.

The people and their chairs had been cleared from the area.

"Is she going to be all right?" asked the mayor.

He slipped his hand below her head, then gently lifted her up off the floor. "It's okay now," he whispered. He held her trembling body against his chest.

"Now what?" Kaira demanded. There had been some kind of disturbance out on the floor and the waiting was driving her crazy.

"Funniest thing I ever saw!" laughed Jerome Paisley as he returned to the backstage area. "This little bit of a girl, wriggling around on the floor, drooling all over herself. She looked like a goldfish that fell out of its bowl. You know how they flop around until they die?"

"You think that's *funny?*" asked Kaira.

"The thing is, everyone thinks she's on drugs, right? But she's not. She was born spastic!"

"And that's *funny?*" asked Kaira again.

"How awful," Kaira's mother said, although she seemed more concerned with her drink, which was now down to nothing but ice.

"See, she was with this big black dude," El Genius explained. "The cops are beating the crap out of him while the little white girl was having a spaz attack, because they thought he gave her drugs!"

"Oh, yeah, that's really funny!" said Kaira. God, she hated him!

"He meant unusual funny, not ha-ha funny," explained her mother.

"That's not how he said it."

"It was their own fault," said her mother's husband. "They paid like three hundred dollars to some scalper for counterfeit tickets!" He laughed. "Some people are too stupid to live!"

"Where are they now?" asked Kaira.

"They should have the area cleared and cleaned up in about five or ten minutes. You better have Rosemary do some touch-up on your hair. It looks a little flat."

"Where are they now?" Kaira asked again.

They were on a cot in the security area, surrounded by a half-dozen security and medical personnel. Armpit still held

Ginny in his arms, but her attack had subsided into tears and hiccups.

The medical personnel were trained to handle drug overdoses and minor injuries, and knew very little about cerebral palsy.

"She doesn't need to go to the hospital," Armpit said. "She just needs space to breathe."

A woman put her hand on Ginny's wrist. "I'm just going to take your pulse."

Ginny jerked her hand away.

The mayor also was there, despite repeated suggestions by the head of security that she return to her seat and enjoy the show. Out in the arena the crowd was calling for Kaira and stomping their feet. Armpit could feel the vibrations on the floor.

"You say he came at you?" the officer in charge asked one of the officers who handcuffed Armpit.

"I was reaching for the ticket!" Armpit tried to explain, then felt Ginny tremble at his sudden outburst.

"He made a threatening movement, but I was able to quickly gain control of the situation."

"There's no question he was resisting arrest," said the other officer.

"His friend was having a seizure!" the mayor pointed out. "He only wanted to help her!"

"Please, Mayor. It would be better for everyone if you returned to your seat."

"I'm not going to let you justify your actions by blaming

the victim," the mayor said firmly. "Let me ask you something," she said, directing her attention to the officer. "Would the gesture have been so threatening if he was white?"

Armpit had to hand it to Cherry Lane. She was one tough lady.

"Instead of persecuting the victim," the mayor went on, "you should be back out there, getting the names and phone numbers of everyone seated in that area. Somebody else may have bought tickets from the same scalper."

Two more people entered the room: a gum-chewing African American teenage girl wearing a lavender sweat suit, followed by a thirty-year-old well-dressed white guy.

"Who the hell are you?" demanded the head of security.

Ginny knew who she was. Her sobs instantly ceased.

"I heard there was a problem with some tickets," the girl said. She sat on the cot next to Armpit and asked Ginny her name.

"Ginny."

"Hi, Ginny."

"Hi, Kaira," said Ginny.

When Armpit realized who she was, he couldn't believe she was sitting right next to him, her leg almost touching his.

"Are you feeling better?" Kaira asked.

"Yes."

"Is she going to be okay?" Kaira asked Armpit.

"She's fine!" Armpit said, sounding a little too

enthusiastic. He couldn't believe he was talking to her. "It's happened before. She just needs a little time and space."

"I hear that," Kaira said to Ginny. "It's a madhouse out there. All these people crowded around, and then they tell you your tickets are no good."

"My body w-went to red alert," said Ginny.

That made Kaira smile. "You seem okay now," she said. "Would you like to come backstage and watch the concert from there?"

"Yes."

16

Armpit wasn't certain if Kaira's invitation included him as well, but he wasn't about to be left behind. Kaira led them out of the security area and down a dark hallway.

"Sorry I walk so slow," said Ginny.

"There's no hurry," said Kaira, as out in the arena the audience was stomping and clapping.

"So are you like her nurse or something?" she asked Armpit.

"We're just friends, that's all," he told her.

"He's my best friend," said Ginny.

"I'm so sorry!" Kaira said. Because Ginny was a white girl, and Armpit was older and an African American, she had just assumed he worked for her family. *Talk about racism!*

Armpit had no idea what she was sorry for.

"This is Fred, my bodyguard," Kaira said. "He's here to protect me from Ginny. You think you can handle her, Fred? She looks awfully dangerous."

Armpit smiled at the joke, but he and everyone else knew Ginny wasn't the one Fred was closely watching.

"Just doin' my job, Miss DeLeon," said Fred.

They reached a flight of stairs and Kaira asked Ginny if she could make it up by herself.

"I need to hold on to someone."

"Hold on to me," said Kaira, extending her hand.

Armpit was amazed by Ginny's calmness. She didn't seem one bit nervous around Kaira DeLeon. He, on the other hand, could hardly think straight.

Kaira led them up a flight of stairs, then through a door and into the backstage area. Several people hurried toward them.

"These are my friends," Kaira said. "Ginny, and . . ."

"Theodore," said Armpit, helping her out.

"We need to set them up somewhere they can see the show." She turned back to Armpit and Ginny. "David will take care of you."

David wore a vest but no shirt. He had red hair, a red beard, and a red hairy chest. Tools of various sorts were attached to his belt and in the many pockets of his vest.

"Come with me," David said as a Hispanic woman led Kaira away. "We'll set you up behind the soundboard."

"Wait, wait, wait," said a very pretty woman in a short skirt and tight T-shirt. "Hold on, honey. Let me get you cleaned up first. David, get them some T-shirts."

The woman introduced herself as Rosemary and brought them to a makeup area, where the three backup singers were smoking.

While she was helping Ginny wash up, David returned with a box of souvenir T-shirts. "What color you want?"

"Red," said Ginny.

"One for him, too," said Rosemary, indicating Armpit.

"I'm fine," said Armpit.

"You're a mess. Now take off your shirt."

David grabbed a couple of folding chairs and led Armpit and Ginny out onto the stage. He walked close enough to the keyboard that he could have played a note.

The audience, which had been yelling and stomping impatiently, suddenly stopped and applauded, glad that at last something was happening.

Ginny squeezed Armpit's hand.

David set up the chairs behind a large piece of electronic equipment. "Don't worry," he said. "You'll be invisible here."

They were near one of the speaker towers, but back behind it, so they wouldn't be blasted by the sound.

The soundboard operator introduced himself as Terry. He wore headphones. The soundboard consisted of a panel of switches, dials, and lights. "This is so the band members can hear themselves and each other," he explained.

"Cool," said Armpit.

David returned a moment later with two souvenir cups filled with lemon-lime soda. He hurried off just as everything went pitch dark, and then the music shook the stage, nearly knocking Armpit out of his chair.

Strobe lights flashed on the various band members, and then a green spotlight settled on Kaira DeLeon.

> *"You've heard she's naughty,*
> *You've heard she's wild.*
> *You've heard she's just*
> *A sweet innocent child!*
>
> *"Well, now's the chance*
> *for you to find out!*
> *'Cause I'm the she*
> *You been hearin' about!"*

It was hard to imagine that this was the same gum-chewing girl he had just met a few minutes earlier. She was dazzlingly beautiful.

> *"You wake up screaming*
> *In the middle of the night*
> *Was it a nightmare?*
> *Or was it too much delight?"*

The floor beneath him bounced with each beat of the drum, and he could feel the bass vibrating right down to his bones. He hoped it wasn't too loud for Ginny, but she just stared at Kaira DeLeon, mesmerized.

> *"Better open your eyes,*
> *If you want to find out,*
> *'Cause I'm the she,*
> *You been dreamin' about!"*

The spotlight on Kaira kept changing colors and her fringed outfit seemed to shimmer and change with each new color.

> *"You been warned of her power,*
> *You been warned of her charm.*
> *They say when she loves you,*
> *She causes bodily harm!*

> *"Well, come a little closer,*
> *If you want to find out,*
> *'Cause I'm the she*
> *They warned you about!"*

If the people in the audience could have come any closer they would not have hesitated. The place was going crazy. Ginny shouted something into Armpit's ear, but he couldn't hear her. It didn't matter. He could feel her excitement.

When the song ended they both stood up and wildly applauded. Kaira looked over at them and smiled.

As the concert went on, the songs changed from fast to slow, from funky to sincere, but Kaira maintained a magical hold over the crowd. Even she could feel it. Normally she shut out the audience as she disappeared into the songs, but it was different tonight. It was almost like the audience was part of the band. She fed off their energy.

"I listen to the radio," she said. "So much of what I hear is filled with anger and hatred. It's like guys think they have to be tough and cruel in order to be a man. To me, a man is someone who is brave enough to love, and to let himself be loved."

Cotton, on drums, pounded out a driving, steady beat, and Kaira ripped into the next song.

> *"Angry Young Man, with your!*
> *Angry Young Heart, and your!*
> *Angry Young Eyes, and your!"*

The drum punctuated each line and drove it home.

> *"Angry young mouth, [BANG!] spewing*
> *Twisted cruel words. [BANG!] 'bout the . . .*
> *People you know, [BANG!] and the!*
> *Money you make, [BANG!] and the!*
> *Women you hurt, [BANG!] with your!*
> *Hateful love."*

116

Armpit had heard the song before, but never with such fire behind it. Now, watching her, hearing her, seeing the passion in her eyes, it almost made him cry. The song could have been about him a couple of years ago, before he went to Camp Green Lake. Although it wasn't really Camp Green Lake that released him from his anger. It was coming home and meeting Ginny.

> *"You'll be a*
> *Sorry old man, with a!*
> *Sorry old heart, and two!*
> *Sorry old eyes, with your!*
> *Sorry old rage, in your*
> *Sorry old cage. . . ."*

She followed that with "Imperfection," and he was reminded of Tatiana. He had forgotten all about her. He was glad he'd ended up going with Ginny instead, and it wasn't just because he got to be up onstage. Just seeing the look on Ginny's face as she stared at Kaira made him very happy.

Kaira started in on "Damsel in Distress," and Armpit grabbed Ginny's arm and told her to listen to the words, but it was hard to pick them out. The music was too loud, the audience was screaming, and the backup singers were singing some kind of counterpoint harmony that kept getting in the way.

117

> *". . . these jewels, these shoes, this dress*
> *A perfect picture of success.*
> *No one would ever guess, Armpit,*
> *A damsel in distress."*

"Did you hear that?" he asked her.

She didn't know what he was talking about.

Of course she didn't. He knew that. He knew he had to be hearing something wrong.

Finally, at the very end of the song everything slowed down. The music got real soft, and the backup singers were silent, and even the audience was hushed. Kaira, under a single spotlight, seemed especially alone and vulnerable as she half sang, half whispered the very last words.

> *"Save me, Armpit.*
> *A damsel in distress."*

At least, that was what he heard.

"So?" Armpit asked Ginny as they both stood and applauded.

"I like that song," said Ginny.

Kaira followed that with the fast-paced "Frying Pan," during which the words seemed to just shoot out of her mouth like bullets.

> *"An overworked, underloved, housewife named*
> *Myra*

Has dinner in the skillet, and a load in the dryer.
When a magazine salesman comes to inquire
If she would like to be a magazine buyer,
One look in his eyes, and she's filled with desire.
She buys a subscription to Time, *and one to*
    Esquire.
'Is there anything else, ma'am, that you require?'
She says, 'Take me out of the frying pan . . .
And into the fire!' "

Armpit was amazed Kaira could get all the words out. There were three more verses, and each seemed to be faster than the one before it.

"Whew!" Kaira exclaimed when the song ended, and the audience laughed and applauded.

"Golly," Kaira said. "So many of these songs seem to be about sex!"

This was greeted by hoots and more applause.

"You'd never guess I'm a virgin."

The crowd went wild over that, and the guitar player made a noise that sounded like he popped a string.

Every part of the concert was carefully planned and scripted, but Kaira had never said that before. The words just came out of her mouth. For once, she was having fun. She turned and waved to Ginny and her friend. Ginny waved back, but her friend looked stunned, like a deer in headlights.

The band launched into the next song.

"I'm gonna take you for a ride,
And we're gonna have some fun!
I'm gonna take . . ."

Armpit and Ginny turned and looked at each other. This had become their song. They rose to their feet and remained standing throughout the song.

"Whoo!" Armpit shouted.

Ginny laughed at him.

He held her hand as she twirled in a circle.

"I ain't never been accused of goin' too slow,
So hang on, baby, and don't let go!

"Oh, I got no rearview mirror,
And none on either side.
Got no rearview mirror,
And none on either side.
Ain't no lookin' back, babe,
When I take you for a ride!"

When the song was over, Kaira announced that she'd like to introduce a couple of friends of hers. To Armpit's horror, she turned to him and Ginny. He had a hard enough time just standing in the front of the room in speech class.

"Come on out," she said, wiggling her finger at them.

Ginny stood up, but Armpit remained glued to his chair.

"You better go," said Terry, the soundboard operator, "or it will just get worse."

Armpit held Ginny's hand as they walked across the stage, but it was hard to say who was helping whom this time.

"These are my friends, Ginny, and . . ."

Armpit thought she'd forgotten his name again, but she remembered at the last second.

". . . Theodore. They almost didn't get to see the show tonight. Some low-life ticket scalper sold them counterfeit tickets."

Everyone booed.

"Well, I guess you ended up with pretty good seats after all, didn't you?"

She held the microphone in front of Ginny.

"Yes," Ginny said, then flinched, startled either by the sound of her amplified voice or by the cheers of the audience.

"So how do you like the show so far?" Kaira asked her.

"It's awesome!" said Ginny, and everyone cheered in agreement.

"How about you?" Kaira asked, holding the microphone in front of Armpit.

He didn't know what to say. "Awesome," he echoed.

No one cheered this time.

"I think it's awesome too," said Kaira. "In fact, I think it's the best damn show I've ever done!"

Cotton rat-a-tatted on the drums in agreement.

"So, Ginny, what's your favorite song?"

Ginny didn't hesitate. " 'Red Alert!' "

"You heard the lady!"

The lead guitar whined like a siren as the house rocked with Kaira's biggest hit.

> *"I hear a w-w-warning sound*
> *Every time you c-c-come around . . ."*

She was dancing around Armpit and Ginny as she sang, and kept looking at Armpit as if he was the one she was singing about.

> *"Should you ch-chance to glance at me,*
> *Threatens my security."*

He didn't know what he was supposed to do.

Ginny was shouting "Red Alert!" right along with the backup singers, although he could only read her lips.

> *"Heart's a-th-thumpin'!*
> *Red Alert!*
> *N-n-nerves a-j-j-jumpin'!*
> *Red Alert!*
> *All I hear is a s-s-siren sound."*

At last Armpit managed to ease his way back to the safety of the soundboard, taking Ginny with him.

> *"All systems are sh-shutting . . .*
> *D-d-d-down!"*

Kaira shouted, "Thank you very much! I love you!" and she and the band left the stage.

The crowd shouted for more, Ginny and Armpit right along with them. The lights remained dark.

After about five minutes they came back out and did "Just Hold On a Little Longer." On the last line, *". . . And then I'll be on my way,"* Kaira blew a kiss to the crowd and once again left the stage.

People continued to shout for more, but this time the house lights came on.

"Good show, Kaira," said Duncan.

Kaira was amazed. He had never said that to her before. None of the band members had. But something special had happened tonight; they could all feel it.

"What do you say we go back out and do one more?" said Tim B.

"Sounds good to me," said Cotton.

Usually once the band was done, they were done. It was a job to them, nothing more. They did the one planned encore, and that was it.

"We've played all the songs we know," Duncan pointed out.

"Then let's play one we don't know," said Billy Goat.

Kaira laughed.

"Sounds good to me," said Cotton. "Any ideas, Kaira?"

"You want to try 'Piece of My Heart'?" Kaira suggested. She had been listening to the Janis Joplin CD and it was her favorite song.

"Let's do it," said Tim B.

The place went crazy when they stepped back out onstage.

"We've played every song we know," Kaira told the raucous crowd. "So now we're going to play one we don't know!"

It just might have been the worst performance ever of that song. Kaira had thought she knew the words, but she kept skipping around to different parts of the song and repeating parts she'd already done as the band struggled to keep up with her.

But nobody cared. It was pure fun, and the audience was having fun right along with them. It was the way rock 'n' roll was meant to be.

Even the cutesy-dootsy backup singers, two of whom had already changed back into jeans, came out, and were screaming at the top of their lungs.

"*TAKE IT!*"
"*Take another little piece*
  of my heart now, baby . . ."

The band tried to improvise a big finish, but in the end, the song just fizzled out.

"God, that was awful!" Kaira said with a laugh amid the thunder of applause, and then she and the band left the stage for good.

17

As an army of workers cleared the stage, unhooking power cords, removing instruments and equipment, Armpit and Ginny were unsure of what they were supposed to do or where they were supposed to go. When they stood up their chairs were taken away. They made sure to hold on to their souvenir cups.

There was no way down except through backstage. Besides, they had to get their regular shirts back from whoever had them. So, holding on to each other, they headed back through the curtain.

It wasn't as crowded as earlier, but the people who were there were in constant motion. Someone shouted, "Watch your back!" as a cart full of electronic equipment was wheeled past and out to a loading dock.

"Ginny!"

It was David, the red-bearded guy wearing the vest and no shirt. "Kaira's looking for you. Here, follow me."

Armpit followed too, and David didn't tell him not to. He led them along a very narrow passageway. As they turned the corner they saw and heard Kaira arguing with a large, athletic-looking black man, while Kaira's bodyguard stood off to the side.

". . . *could have* been your best performance," the man was saying, "but you know what the critics are going to write? 'She's no Janis Joplin.' All they're going to talk about is how you butchered her classic song!"

"We were having fun! Rock 'n' roll is supposed to be spontaneous!"

"Where'd you hear that?"

"Cotton."

"Cotton," the man repeated. He glanced at Armpit and Ginny. "This area is off limits," he said.

"They're my friends!" said Kaira. "I invited them."

The man scowled, then turned and walked away.

"Sorry about that," Kaira said. "So, you guys want some ice cream?"

"Yes," said Ginny.

"Uh, what flavor?" asked Armpit. He didn't know why he said that. Sometimes words seemed to come out of his mouth on their own.

"I'll check," Kaira said. She opened the door to her dressing room and went inside.

Armpit and Ginny remained in the hall.

"Well, come in," Kaira said to them, as if she thought they were being stupid.

Ginny entered, followed by Armpit.

Kaira's bodyguard started to come in as well, but Kaira told him to wait outside.

Armpit was surprised by how small the room was—not much bigger than a utility closet. A small couch had been squeezed in between two walls, and a miniature refrigerator sat on the floor across from it.

Kaira opened the tiny refrigerator, and the even tinier freezer compartment, which was just big enough to hold a quart of ice cream. "It's chocolate chip," she told Armpit. "Is that okay?"

"Sure, fine," Armpit said, wishing he had never asked about the flavor.

"I can ask David to get you something else."

"Chocolate chip is my favorite ice cream!" he said, trying to put an end to the subject but instead sounding like a little kid.

Kaira scooped the ice cream into two plastic bowls and gave them each one. "Well, sit down."

"You should get the couch," said Armpit. "You're the star."

"Shut up," said Kaira.

Ginny laughed. "She told you to shut up."

"I know. I heard her."

Armpit sat on the couch next to Ginny. Kaira sat on the floor and ate her ice cream right out of the carton.

"I always get so hungry after a show," she said. "Before the show I'm too nervous to eat."

"You didn't seem nervous," said Armpit. "You seemed really cool."

Kaira laughed. "Cool? Look at me. I'm drenched in sweat. It's gross!"

If Armpit knew her better he might have said, *You think you're sweaty. Man, you don't know what sweat is!* But he didn't dare say that to Kaira DeLeon.

"Why was that man y-yelling at you?" Ginny asked.

"Him? That's El—my manager," Kaira said. "He's all pissed off 'cause of the last song. Oh, sorry, Ginny."

"It's okay," said Ginny. "I h-hear b-bad words at school."

"I thought that last song was great!" Armpit said.

"Well, I don't know about that," said Kaira.

"Is it a new one?" Armpit asked her.

"You never heard it before?"

"No."

"Don't tell me you've never heard of Janis Joplin?"

He hadn't, but he didn't dare admit it now. "Maybe I have," he said.

"If you'd heard her, you'd know. She's like my all-time favorite singer. You know, she was born right here in Texas."

"Have you met her?" asked Ginny.

"We're all going to meet Janis someday," said Kaira. "But

it won't be in Texas." She turned back to Armpit. "Have you heard of the Beatles?"

"Shut up," he said.

Ginny gasped, but Kaira only laughed.

"So what grade are you in, Ginny?" Kaira asked.

"F-fourth. I was in fourth. I'm g-going into f-fifth."

"Fifth grade's great," said Kaira. "What about you? Are you still in school?"

"I'll sort of be a senior in high school."

"Oh, yeah? What sort of senior will you be?"

"He missed a year," Ginny explained. "He w-was at Camp Green Lake."

"She doesn't need to know about that," said Armpit.

"What's Camp Green Lake?"

"It's nothing," said Armpit.

"A juvenile correctional facility," Ginny said, carefully pronouncing each word.

"You mean like a jail?" asked Kaira.

"It's a long story," Armpit said. "Four years ago I got in a fight and things got out of hand, and so I was sent to a kind of work camp for a year. And now I'm having to take summer school to try to catch up."

He wondered if Kaira now regretted shutting the door on her bodyguard.

"Can I tell her your nickname?" asked Ginny.

"No."

Kaira smiled. "What's his nickname?"

"Don't tell her, Ginny."

"Ginny?" coaxed Kaira.

"You better not," Armpit warned her.

"Come here, Ginny," said Kaira. "I want to tell you a secret."

Ginny slid off the couch, and Kaira whispered something in her ear. Then Ginny whispered something into Kaira's ear. They both looked at Armpit. Then Kaira whispered something to Ginny, and Ginny whispered something to Kaira.

Armpit didn't like it one bit. And he didn't like the way Kaira and Ginny smiled conspiratorially at each other either, when Ginny returned to the couch.

"You told her, didn't you?"

Ginny shook her head,

"She didn't tell me," Kaira said. She winked at Ginny. Ginny shut, then opened both eyes.

There was a knock at the door.

"Go away!" Kaira shouted.

The door opened anyway and a bald-headed black man entered. Armpit recognized the drummer.

"Oh, I didn't know it was you," Kaira said apologetically. "These are my friends, Ginny and Theodore. This is Cotton, our drummer."

"Well, not anymore," said Cotton. "Your dad just fired me. I just wanted to stop in and say good-bye."

"He can't do that!"

"He can, and he did."

"But I'm the one who wanted to sing that song!" Kaira said.

"Hey, don't worry. I'm cool with it. This really isn't the kind of music I should be making at this time in my life. I need to do something real."

"He's not my dad," Kaira said. "Just because he married my— As soon as I turn eighteen I'm firing his ass! Then I'll call you."

"You do that," Cotton said. "Nice to meet you," he said to Ginny and Armpit without looking at them, then left the dressing room.

"That sucks," Kaira said.

"Sorry," said Ginny.

"Yeah, me too," Kaira said. She sat in silence for a moment.

"Maybe we should go," Armpit said to Ginny.

"You know what I do all day?" Kaira asked. "I watch TV and play video games. All day."

That didn't sound too bad to him.

"I have no friends. But then finally, finally I find someone I can talk to. Someone I like. And so of course El Genius has to fire him. I swear that's the reason he was fired. Not because we did that song. Because he was someone I could talk to."

Armpit could only follow about half of what she was saying. "We really ought to get going," he said. "Ginny's mom will worry."

Kaira turned to Ginny. "You like your mom?" she asked.

"Yes."

132

"You're lucky," Kaira said. "How about you?" she asked Armpit.

"Yeah, I like Ginny's mom," said Armpit.

Kaira laughed. "You're funny. Man, you guys are so cool. It's so great you can be such good friends, when, you know, you're so different. I mean, different ages."

"Different colors, too," said Ginny.

Kaira went nose to nose with Ginny and said, "Well, *duh*!"

"Duh!" Ginny repeated, right back at her.

There was another knock on the door, and this time it was David with their shirts, washed, dried, and neatly folded.

It was hard for Armpit to imagine this big, red-bearded guy washing their shirts.

Kaira gave Ginny a good-bye hug. Armpit wouldn't have minded one of those himself, but he just shrugged and said, "Well, see ya."

"See ya," said Kaira.

"So what did you and Kaira whisper to each other?" he asked when they got back to the car.

"It's a secret," Ginny said.

"You're not going to tell me?"

"No."

"You're really not going to tell me?"

"No."

"After I take you to this concert and everything, you won't even tell me? Now I'm mad."

"Are you really mad?" asked Ginny.

"No."

"I didn't think you were."

"You didn't tell her my nickname, did you?"

"I j-just g-gave her a hint."

"A hint? What kind of a hint?"

"I said it was a p-part of the b-body."

"That's even worse!" He could just imagine what she was imagining. "Well, I guess it doesn't really matter," he said. "It's not like I'll ever see her again."

"Yes, you will," said Ginny.

"Oh, I will, will I?"

"Maybe."

18

"Do you realize it's after midnight?"

"That's how long concerts last."

"Then you should have left early."

"In the middle of the concert?"

"Yes! You had a responsibility to Ginny, and to her mother. You have no idea how worried she was! She was ready to call the police!"

Armpit knew that wasn't true. He had just come from Ginny's mother, who was delighted that Ginny had had such a wonderful time.

"The best time of my whole life!" Ginny had said.

They had told her about having ice cream with Kaira DeLeon, but not about the counterfeit tickets. They just said that Ginny had gotten a little overexcited and suffered a mild seizure. She was taken to the medical station, where they met Kaira DeLeon, and so on.

Armpit didn't tell any of that to his own parents. He felt like he was under attack the second he walked in the door, and so didn't tell them anything except his name, rank, and serial number.

He didn't have to work Sundays and would have slept late, but shortly after nine someone turned on his bedroom light. He shielded his eyes as X-Ray smiled down on him.

"What are you doing here?" His voice was a little bit hoarse from the night before.

"Your mom let me in. Said it served you right for staying out so late."

When he and X-Ray were at Camp Green Lake together, they were forced to get up every morning at four-thirty. X-Ray always said that he'd sleep until noon every day once he was released, but his internal clock was permanently out of whack. It had been more than two years since his release, and he still couldn't stay in bed past six-thirty.

"So I guess you got to see the concert," X-Ray said. "If you were out so late?"

The last bit of sleep slowly cleared from Armpit's brain, and the memory of the night before came back to him. "I'm going to kill you," he told X-Ray.

"Maybe your seats weren't quite as good, but at least you got to see the show, right? No harm, no foul. Right?"

Armpit sat up and placed one foot on the floor. "First I'm going to put my pants on, and then I'm going to kill you."

The pants he'd worn the night before were on the floor of his room. "That's one leg," he said as he stepped into it.

"Wait, now just hold on a second. I got something here that just might cool your jets." X-Ray reached into his pocket and pulled out a wad of money. "Two hundred and ninety-eight dollars!"

"My pants are on," Armpit said, then slowly moved toward X-Ray, backing him against the wall.

"Look, I had to make a business decision," X-Ray said. "You weren't there, so I had to do what I thought was right."

Armpit grabbed him by the collar. "What you thought was *right*? You thought you were doing *the right thing*?"

"Look, what was I supposed to do? You kept calling me back, changing your mind. Sell the tickets. No, don't sell the tickets, I'm taking Tatiana. No, I'm not taking Tatiana. Sell 'em. No, don't sell 'em, I'm taking Ginny."

"And that's the last thing I said," said Armpit, shaking X-Ray on each word: "Don't . . . sell . . . the . . . tickets!"

"And I heard you," said X-Ray. "I heard you. But I already agreed to meet the dude at the H-E-B. That's the least I can do is still meet him, right? I can't disrespect him. So I get there, and I'm waiting in the parking lot, and I'm thinking, if only there was some way you and Ginny could go to the concert, and I could sell the tickets. And then suddenly, right in front of me is a big sign: *All Your Copying Needs*. I'm telling you, it was like a sign from God! I mean, how many times have I been to the H-E-B without noticing there was a Copy King right there? Did you know it was there?"

"God musta put it there just for you," said Armpit.

"So I go inside, but just to look around. Just to see what's *possible*, if you know what I'm saying. They had all different kinds of paper, and so I hold a ticket against the paper, comparing, you know, trying to find the right thickness. And then I made some copies—but just to see how they'd look, I swear! I wasn't planning to do anything with them.

"Then I got back outside, and the guy shows up, and I told him the tickets were no longer for sale. I did. I told him that. But he says he's desperate. He offers me two hundred and fifty apiece. Sorry, I promised them to a friend. Three hundred? I mean, what am I supposed to do? I mean now we're talking a total of six hundred!"

Armpit glared at him.

"You weren't there. I had to make a decision. Look, I thought you'd figure out what to do when you saw people in your seats."

"We got there first," said Armpit.

"That's impossible! I waited before coming to your house."

"So you just came over, handed me the tickets, without even a warning."

"I warned you. I told you to be flexible."

"Oh, I was flexible, all right. I had both arms stretched behind my back!"

"I was afraid you'd blow it," said X-Ray. "You're not a

very good liar. You look all guilty and nervous and I was afraid you'd never make it past the ticket taker. But if you didn't know, you'd just waltz right in. I didn't want to disappoint Ginny."

Armpit grabbed him by the neck and lifted him off the floor.

The door to his room opened. He let go of X-Ray and backed away as his mother entered.

"You have a phone call."

"Uh, thanks." He took the phone from her, and she walked out. He hoped she hadn't seen the money on the bed.

"Hello?"

"Hi. I hope it's not too early."

"Uh, no, I just got up."

"We don't have to leave for Dallas until one. You want to get together and have breakfast or something?"

"Sure, that would be great."

"Cool! I'm staying at the Four Seasons. It's next to a river or lake or something. If you want I can look up the address."

"No, I know where it is," said Armpit. He had seen it from the bus.

"Oh, and when you come, don't ask for Kaira DeLeon. You have to ask for Samantha Stevens."

"Is that your real name?"

"Yeah, I'm a witch." She laughed. "No, I always check in under a fake name. Have you ever watched that old TV show *Bewitched*?"

"Is that the one with the genie?"

"No, dummy, the one with the witch! It's not called *Begenied*!"

Armpit told her he'd be there in forty-five minutes. He had to shower first.

He hung up, then walked over to the bed and scooped up the money. "Two hundred and ninety-eight dollars?"

"It cost four dollars to make the copies. I figured we'd split it."

Armpit stared at him.

"Okay, fine," said X-Ray. He tossed in another two bucks. "So who was that?"

"Kaira DeLeon. Can you give me a ride to the Four Seasons? I'm supposed to meet her for breakfast."

19

X-Ray's car was parked out front facing the wrong way. He opened the only door that worked, then slid over to the driver's side. "So really, where are we going?" he asked as Armpit got in beside him.

"The Four Seasons."

"Right, because Kaira DeLeon wants to have breakfast with you."

"Yes," said Armpit.

He didn't tell him anything more. It was his payback for the phony tickets.

The whole way there, X-Ray kept glancing sideways at him, trying to see a hint of a smile, or some kind of clue, but Armpit remained cool, as if nothing was out of the ordinary.

The X-Mobile turned off Cesar Chavez Avenue and into

the hotel's circular driveway. A doorman opened Armpit's door for him.

"Excuse me," X-Ray said to him. "Is Kaira DeLeon staying here?"

"I wouldn't know, sir."

"Yes, you would. She's not here. You'd know if she was here."

Armpit thanked X-Ray for the ride, then walked through the revolving door into the hotel.

The inside of the hotel reminded Armpit of pictures he'd seen of ancient Greek temples, with stone pillars and marble floors. He had no idea where he was supposed to go. The concierge seemed too intimidating, so he asked one of the bellhops, who directed him to the house phone.

Armpit picked up the receiver and dialed zero.

"How may I direct your call?" the operator asked him.

He hung up.

He'd forgotten the name she'd given him. It was the lady from *Bewitched*, he knew that, but he couldn't remember her name. He could picture her perfectly, and could even hear the musical notes they played whenever she twitched her nose. Mary? Mindy? He was pretty sure it started with an "M."

A family of four came out of the elevator and headed in his direction. They all had blond hair. The husband could have been a tennis pro, and the wife looked like a model. The girls were twins, about seven or eight years old.

"Excuse me," Armpit said. "You ever watch the show *Bewitched?*" He knew he must have sounded crazy.

The father crossed in front of his daughters to protect them. He would have kept on going, hurrying his family along, but the mother stopped.

"What about it?" she asked.

"Do you remember the name of the woman, you know, the one who was the witch?"

She tried to remember. They all did.

"Elizabeth Montgomery," said the father.

"That doesn't sound right," said Armpit.

"I'm sure," said the father.

"That's the name of the actress," Armpit realized. "I need the name of the person on the show. You know, the name of the character."

"Oh, I thought you wanted the name of the actress," the father said, disappointed not to have been given the credit he thought he deserved.

"Her husband's name was Darren," said the wife.

"Samantha," said one of the girls.

"That's right!" said her mother. "Darren called her Sam, but her name was Samantha. Very good, Ashley."

"Do you remember her last name, Ashley?" Armpit asked the girl.

"Stevens," the father declared proudly. "Samantha Stevens."

"Thanks." Armpit picked up the phone and asked the operator for Samantha Stevens.

The blond family stared at him. "Is she staying at this hotel?" asked the father.

Five minutes later Kaira DeLeon stepped off the elevator, along with Fred, her bodyguard. Kaira wore denim shorts and a sleeveless top that stopped above her belly button. Her yellow toenails matched her flip-flops.

"How ya doin', Knuckles?" she greeted him.

"Hi," he said.

"Was that it?" she asked. "Is Knuckles your name?"

"No, I didn't even get what you said."

"Is it Elbow?"

"I'm not going to tell you even if you guess it."

"It's Elbow."

"It's not Elbow."

Despite the weather, Fred was wearing a tan sports coat over a black T-shirt. He looked very stylish. If Armpit didn't know better, he would have guessed that he was the rich and famous one of the two.

"You hungry?" Kaira asked.

"Starving!" he said, and he had been, until he saw her. Now he was too nervous.

"The café here is really good."

She led the way down a flight of stairs. The hotel had been built on the side of a hill, so even though they went down, the café was still on ground level, with an outdoor patio overlooking the river.

"Three?" asked the hostess.

"Two," said Kaira. "And we don't want to sit too close to him either."

On the way to their table they passed the blond family seated at a booth. All four smiled and waved to Armpit like they were old friends. He waved back.

"You know them?" asked Kaira, more than a little surprised.

"Sort of."

They were seated at a table in the corner. Fred's table was far enough away to give them privacy but close enough for him to come to her aid, just in case.

A waiter came by with coffee and fresh-squeezed orange juice. Kaira had coffee but no juice. Armpit had just the opposite.

"Muscles?" said Kaira.

"I'm not going to tell you either way."

She dumped a packet of sugar into her coffee, then another one, and then a third.

"So you like sugar in your coffee," he said.

He felt awkward. They both did.

He was glad when the waitress brought them their menus so he had something to focus on. And when he saw the prices he was glad X-Ray had brought over the three hundred dollars. There was nothing on the menu for less than twenty dollars, and that included cereal.

"Toenail?" asked Kaira.

He didn't answer.

The waitress returned. Kaira ordered lemon ricotta pancakes, and he ordered corned-beef hash and eggs.

"How'd you get my phone number?" he asked her.

"David got it for me, from security."

"David," said Armpit. "He was the guy with the vest."

"What?"

"He wore a vest and no shirt."

"I didn't notice," said Kaira. "So what was it like at that camp? Was it hard?"

"Yeah."

"What'd you do there?"

"Dug holes."

"That all?"

"Pretty much. Every day another hole."

Kaira nodded as if she understood, but he knew she didn't.

"You like being a famous singer?" he asked her. It was a stupid question, and he wished he hadn't asked it.

"It's all right," she said.

They sat in silence for a moment. It had been a lot easier to talk to each other when Ginny was there.

"Have you seen the view from the patio?" she asked him.

"No."

"You need to see the view," she said, in a voice that seemed unusually loud. "You can see the lake."

"It's actually a river," he said.

"Whatever," said Kaira.

"There's a huge colony of bats living under a bridge right by here," he told her.

"Bats?" Kaira said, again in an unusually loud voice. "Let's go look at the bats."

"You're not going to be able to see them now," Armpit said, but she was already out of her seat. "They only come out at night."

"We'll just look from the patio," Kaira said again rather loudly.

She was talking to him, but he got the feeling that everything she said was for Fred's benefit.

He followed her through the sliding glass doors out to the patio. A well-manicured lawn gently sloped away from the patio and down to a walkway. On the other side of the walkway the hill got much steeper and led down to the river.

"Nice view," he said.

Kaira took off her flip-flops. "Do you want to play ditch the Doofus?"

"What?"

She stepped off the patio and raced across the lawn.

For a second he was afraid he was the doofus, but then he remembered that was what she called her bodyguard. He watched her leap over the concrete walkway and disappear down the hill.

He took off after her but lost control as he headed down the steepest part of the slope. "Look out!" he shouted at Kaira, who was now standing on a dirt path beside the river.

As he tried to put on the brakes, she grabbed hold of his

arm, and together they spun around three hundred and sixty degrees.

Kaira's face bounced hard against his shoulder.

"You all right?"

She laughed.

"That was close," Armpit said.

Kaira smiled at him as she let her palm slide down his arm, then held his hand.

They walked along the dirt path, continuing to hold hands. "So you're not worried I'll try to kill you now that you ditched your bodyguard?"

"You?" asked Kaira. "Are you kidding? You're such a wimp."

Armpit pointed out the bridge with the bats.

"I don't like bats," said Kaira. "They're creepy."

"So, like has Fred ever had to save your life or anything?" he asked her.

"All you talk about is the Doofus!"

"I was just curious."

"Mostly he just keeps people from getting too close to me. Of course, it kind of makes it hard to meet guys. I mean, what guy wants to go out with a girl and her bodyguard? You try to kiss her and you risk getting your head blown off."

Did she squeeze his hand when she said the word "kiss"? If she did, it wasn't a big squeeze. Just a little twinge.

What he should have said was "I'll risk it," and then

kissed her. That would have been really smooth, but by the time he thought of it, it was too late. The timing was off.

They continued along the river.

"I get all kinds of weird letters," said Kaira. "I've gotten seven marriage proposals! One guy claims to be a billionaire Arab prince."

"You think he really is?"

"Why, you want to marry him?" asked Kaira.

Armpit laughed.

"They're all freakazoids. There's this one who calls himself Billy Boy, you know, like that song." She sang very softly: *"Oh, where have you been, Billy Boy, Billy Boy? Oh, where have you been, charming Billy?"*

Hearing her voice while holding her hand was almost too much for him to take.

"He wants to marry you?" asked Armpit.

"No, he wants to kill me."

"Really?"

"Seriously. He's written like five letters so far, saying he's going to break my pretty little neck. I even got one at this hotel."

Armpit couldn't help looking around behind him.

Kaira laughed. "It's so lame," she said. "He even cuts out little letters and glues them to the paper."

"You're not scared?"

"You'll protect me."

"Me? I'm a wimp."

"So tell me about you," said Kaira. "What are your big dreams? I mean, besides wanting to marry an Arab prince?"

"I don't have big dreams," Armpit said. "I just take small steps."

He told her about the advice the counselor at the halfway house had given to him. The important thing was to take small steps and just keep on moving forward. "Life is like crossing a river. If you try to take too big a step, the current will knock you off your feet and carry you away."

"That's kind of poetic," said Kaira.

"I didn't make it up," said Armpit.

"My manager tells me I need to take big steps," she said. "I have to grab for everything I can get right now, because in a few years I could be all washed up."

"I doubt that," said Armpit.

"There's this song I'm writing." She sang again: *Britney Spears is old and gray—she turned twenty-five today.* That's really all I've got so far."

"You write your own songs?"

"A couple. I wrote 'Angry Young Man' and 'Damsel in Distress.' "

For a brief second he thought about asking her the words to "Damsel in Distress" but then thought better of it. It could only lead to his embarrassment.

"And then El Genius—that's what my manager calls himself, El Genius—he had people kind of fix them up and arrange the music. He's such a control freak. Sometimes I

150

think he's the one who's sending me the Billy Boy letters, just so he can have even more control over me. It's an excuse for having the Doofus watch me all the time. He's also married to my mother."

"Your bodyguard?"

"No, my manager. But I bet he just married her to have more control over me, because he's got a girlfriend, too. It doesn't matter. I'm going to fire him when I turn eighteen."

Armpit could only shake his head in wonder. She lived in such a different world.

"You've got nice strong hands," said Kaira.

"They're all calloused from digging."

"Is that your name? Hands?"

"No."

"Fingers? Are you the middle finger?"

Armpit dropped her hand. "I'll tell you what. I'll make you a deal. I'll tell you my name, but on one condition."

"What?"

"Whatever my name is, you have to touch me there."

Kaira took a step backward. "I have to touch you there."

"That's the deal."

She slowly looked him over, starting at his feet and working her way upward. "Ginny said it wasn't anyplace nasty."

Armpit shrugged.

"You are so mean."

"Do you want to know or don't you?"

"Okay, tell me."

"Do we have a deal?"

"Yes, we have a deal."

Armpit waited a long moment, then quietly said, "Armpit."

Kaira shrieked, causing several other walkers to turn and look at them.

"You are so bad," Kaira said. "Oh, you are so bad. Okay, raise up your elbow."

He did so.

She slowly moved her finger up the sleeve of his T-shirt, but he suddenly laughed and pulled away.

"You're ticklish!"

She tried again, but again he couldn't stay still.

"Are you going to let me do this or not? Close your eyes."

He did so and waited. She held on to his shoulder. It was hard to keep still.

She quickly poked her finger up his sleeve and fulfilled her part of the bargain.

He opened his eyes.

"Yuck, it's all sweaty," she said as she wiped her finger on her shorts.

He started to explain about the scorpion but she wasn't interested. Her hand was still on his left shoulder, and now she placed her other hand on the right one.

He gently held her waist and felt her rise to her tiptoes.

He could feel blood pulsating against the tips of his fingers but couldn't tell if it was his or hers.

He leaned toward her.

"What are you doing?" she exclaimed, suddenly backing away.

"My job, Miss DeLeon," said a voice behind him.

20

"So you d-didn't kiss her?"

"I couldn't. Not with her bodyguard right there."

"I would have kissed her," said Ginny.

"*You* would have kissed her?" Armpit teased.

Ginny giggled at that. "I m-mean if I was you. If I was a b-b-boy."

Armpit ate a spoonful of Cheerios. They were in her half of the house. They were her Cheerios.

He knew Ginny was right. How many chances in your life do you get to kiss someone like Kaira DeLeon? He'd thought about nothing else since the moment Fred showed up.

Fred had ruined the moment, but as the three of them headed back to the hotel, Armpit had had it all planned out. Just before saying good-bye, he would say something smooth like "Next time you're in town, give me a call," and then kiss her.

But it never happened. Kaira's manager was in the hotel lobby when she returned, and she started yelling at him for firing the drummer, and he told her that drummers were a dime a dozen. Kaira was practically in tears. She told Armpit she was "sorry about all this," then went sulking off into the elevator.

"She told me to say hi to you."

"She did?"

"Yeah. She thinks you're really cool."

Ginny smiled. Her glasses slid down her nose and she pushed them back in place.

"What happened to the f-food?"

"What food?"

"At the café."

Armpit laughed because he had wondered about that too. After Kaira went up in the elevator, he went back to the restaurant to check.

"They threw it away."

"Too bad," said Ginny.

"Yeah, I woulda liked to have tried those twenty-nine-dollar eggs."

"Did you have to pay for them?"

"No, everything was charged to her room, but it's not like she pays for it either. Everything's charged to the tour. It's a whole other world. It's no big deal to them to pay a hundred dollars for breakfast."

155

"No wonder t-tickets cost so much," said Ginny.

"You're right."

A car parked in front of their house and a young white woman got out. They watched her through the front window as she stepped onto the porch.

"You know her?" Armpit asked.

"No."

Skin color was usually a reliable indicator as to which half of the house a visitor was heading for, but this woman was the exception to the rule. She checked her small notebook, then knocked on Armpit's front door.

"Maybe Kaira sent her," said Ginny.

He had been hoping the same thing. He went to the door. "May I help you?"

The woman turned around. "I'm looking for Theodore Johnson."

"I'm Theodore."

The woman checked the address on the door.

"You're right. That's were I live," Armpit explained. "I'm just over here right now."

"Oh, then I guess you're Ginny McDonald."

"Yes," Ginny said, at Armpit's side.

The woman took a black wallet from her purse. "I'm Detective Debbie Newberg from the Austin Police Department." She opened the wallet, showing them her badge. "I wanted to talk to you about the concert tickets."

Armpit struggled to keep his composure. "You want to talk to both of us, or just me?" he asked.

156

"Were you with him when he bought the tickets?" she asked Ginny.

"No."

"Then just you, if you don't mind."

Armpit went out one door and in the other. He led Detective Newberg into the living room and offered her something to drink, but she declined. He sat at one end of the red and blue plaid couch, and she sat across from him on an ottoman, her knees close together and her notebook on her lap.

She seemed too young and too pretty to be a police officer. She had bright brown eyes, and curly black hair very similar to Kaira's. Her cheeks had a red glow to them, as if she was blushing.

"So I understand you paid six hundred dollars for the tickets, is that correct?"

He hated to start right out with a lie, but it was the path of least resistance. "Yes, ma'am."

"Was that six hundred total, or six hundred per ticket?"

"Total," he said. "Three hundred per ticket."

"That's a lot of money."

He suddenly felt very conscious of the old and well-worn furniture. Everything in his house seemed shoddy and cheap.

"Well, I wasn't planning to pay that much," he said. "It was supposed to be only a hundred and thirty-five a ticket, but then the guy kept changing his mind. First they were for sale. Then they weren't. Then they were again. Three hundred's not really that much for Kaira DeLeon tickets. They went for seven hundred and fifty in Philadelphia."

"Wow," said Detective Newberg.

He tried to relax. He wasn't a suspect, he reminded himself. He was the victim. She was here to help him.

"What do you mean they were only *supposed to cost* one hundred and thirty-five?"

"There was an ad in the paper."

The second he said that, he knew it was a mistake. She could easily get ahold of last week's newspapers and find the ad, along with X-Ray's phone number.

"What newspaper was that?" she asked.

"It wasn't really a newspaper. It was one of those free advertisements, you know, that they stick on your door."

"Do you still have it?"

"No, it got recycled."

"Do you remember what day it was placed on your door?"

"No. It might have been two weeks ago. I just don't remember."

"And the ad was for a hundred and thirty-five dollars?"

"No, I don't think it was that much."

"You just said—"

"It was for ninety-five," Armpit said firmly. "But that was two weeks ago. By the time I called the guy, he said the price had gone up to a hundred and thirty-five so I told him I had to think about it. Then when I called him back on the day of the concert, he said the tickets were no longer for sale. But then he called me back and said they were for sale again, but the price was now two hundred. But then when I tried to buy the tickets he said they weren't for sale again."

"And that's when you offered him three hundred?"

Armpit nodded. "I was desperate. It was five-thirty. The concert was at eight. I'd already promised Ginny."

"Did he ever tell you his name?"

He shook his head.

"It wasn't in the ad?"

"No," said Armpit. "Look, why— I mean, what's the big deal? Ginny and I ended up getting to sit on the stage. You know—no harm, no foul?"

"Well, our mayor seems to think there was quite a bit of harm. She saw what happened to Ginny, and to you, and she wants to get the guy."

"What will happen to him?" Armpit asked, trying to sound only mildly curious. "Will he have to go to jail?"

"Oh, I doubt it. We're just talking six hundred dollars."

He tried not to let his relief show on his face.

"Unless he has a prior criminal record," said Detective Newberg.

Armpit sat up straight.

"So your initial contact with him was by phone?"

It took Armpit a moment to decipher the question. "Um, yes."

"I don't suppose you remember his phone number?"

"No."

She smiled. Her cheeks turned pink. "I wouldn't expect you to. So then, where did you meet him?"

"At H-E-B. In the parking lot."

"And how did you recognize each other?"

"I didn't. I never saw him before in my life."

Detective Newberg raised her eyebrows. "What I'm asking is, how did you find each other in the parking lot? How did you know he was the one selling the tickets?"

"Oh." Armpit noticed his Raincreek cap hanging on the back of the door. "I said I'd be wearing a red cap."

He got up and got the cap. It felt good to get up and move around.

He showed her the cap, but she didn't seem all that interested. He put the cap on his head. "So then he drove up beside me, and we bargained a little, like I said, and then I gave him the money, and he gave me the tickets." He sat back down on the arm of the couch. He removed the cap and set it on the cushion beside him.

"What kind of car was he driving?"

"A white Suburban."

"And where were you standing?"

"On the curb."

"In front of the H-E-B?"

"No, a few stores over. I think it was in front of Copy King."

Why did he say that? Sometimes it felt like the words just jumped out of his mouth.

"Was he the only one in the car?"

"Yeah."

"So he was driving on the wrong side of the road."

"He was?"

"If the driver's side was next to the curb."

"Oh, yeah, I guess so," said Armpit. He realized he had to be more careful. "I didn't notice because there weren't any other cars around."

"At five-thirty?" asked Detective Newberg. "Man, I should start shopping there!" She smiled. "The H-E-B by me is jammed that time of day."

Armpit shrugged.

"So what did he look like?"

"I didn't get a real good look."

"You were face to face, weren't you, when he rolled down his window?"

"I was thinking about the tickets, not what he looked like."

"Was he white? Black? Hispanic?"

"Kind of black."

"Kind of black?"

"I think he might have been Iranian."

Iranian? Where did that come from?

"You think he was Iranian?"

"Maybe part black, part Iranian," Armpit said. "Now I remember. He said his name was Habib. That's why I think he's part Iranian."

Officer Newberg raised her eyebrows. "Habib?" She wrote the name in her little black notebook.

"Did he speak with an accent?"

"Um, yeah, kind of."

161

"An Iranian accent?"

"Yeah."

"Was he tall? Short? Thin? Fat?"

"Kind of big," Armpit said. "But it was hard to tell because he was sitting down in his car."

"How old?"

"Maybe about your age."

"How old do you think I am?"

He studied her face. "Twenty-three?"

"I'm twenty-eight." She smiled. "So we'll say he's in his twenties. Any distinguishing characteristics?"

"No."

"Tattoos? Facial hair?"

"Oh, yeah. He had a mustache."

"Nice of you to mention it."

"I didn't think it was important. I mean, he probably shaved it off by now, don't you think?"

She shrugged. "Anything else come to mind?"

He shook his head.

"You sure?"

"Not that I remember."

"Okay, well, this is a good start. I'm going to talk to some of the other people seated nearby at the concert. Maybe they also bought their tickets from Habib."

She gave him a card with her name and phone number on it and told him to call her if he remembered anything else.

He shook her hand. It felt cool and soft.

As he watched her drive away, he felt bad about having to lie to her. She was nice. She had a sweet smile. It was hard to imagine her out in the world, fighting criminals. He worried she might get hurt.

21

X-Ray paced back and forth by his car, which was parked in front of Armpit's house. "We got nothing to worry about," he said. "Nothing to worry about. The police have better things to do than to launch a big investigation over a couple of phony tickets."

Armpit had told him everything, including how he had met Kaira.

"Man, I wish you had talked to me first," X-Ray said. "I could have come up with something believable."

"I think she believed me," said Armpit.

"*Habib?*" X-Ray shook his head. "And you never should have mentioned the H-E-B."

"Yeah, I wasn't thinking."

"Well, that's obvious. Look, if she interrogates you

164

again, just remember one word: 'kiss.' K-I-S-S. Keep It Simple, Stupid!"

"I think she believed me."

"You know we're in this together. We split the money, fifty-fifty."

Yes, he realized that.

"Not to worry," X-Ray said. "The cops have better things to do. Man, it's just my luck the mayor was at the concert! What kind of mayor goes to rock concerts?"

"You're lucky she was there," Armpit pointed out.

"Oh, yeah? How's that?"

"If the mayor wasn't there, I woulda been sent to jail, Ginny woulda been taken to a hospital and had her stomach pumped, and you'd be dead."

X-Ray laughed. "You're such a joker."

At school on Monday, Tatiana wanted to know all about the concert. "You still went, didn't you?"

"Oh, I had a great time. Too bad you missed it."

"Were you able to find someone to go with you?"

"Yeah, that wasn't a problem."

"A girl?"

He nodded.

"Well, good. I'm really glad you had such a good time!"

"She wore this thing with long white fringe—"

"You know what?" said Tatiana. "I really don't care what your girlfriend was wearing."

"My girlfriend? No, you asked me to tell you what Kaira DeLeon had on."

"I don't have time for this now," Tatiana said, then walked away.

In economics he gave Matt Kapok the dollar back.

Matt seemed surprised. "Uh, thanks, Arm—" His white face turned even whiter. "I mean, I mean, I mean, Theodore. Thanks, Theodore."

"You really helped me out," Armpit said. "I owe you one."

On the back of their souvenir T-shirts was a list of the fifty-four cities on the tour. Ginny and Armpit looked at them every day for the next week and a half and tried to predict where Kaira was.

"Maybe she'll call from Albuquerque," said Ginny, studying the T-shirt. "Al-bu-quer-que," she repeated. She liked saying that word.

Armpit laughed. "She's not going to call," he said, as if he never gave it a thought, when in truth it was practically all he'd thought about since he'd last seen her. Every time the phone rang his body went to red alert. He hated leaving the house for school or work because he was afraid he might miss her call. But after a week and a half, that didn't seem too likely anymore.

"It's like she says in her song," he told Ginny. "She'll get around to you, and then she'll be on her way."

He just wished he could have held on a little bit longer.

He had failed a quiz in economics earlier that day. He hadn't read the last two chapters. He couldn't concentrate.

At work the day before he'd installed a sprinkler system in the front yard of a house. Jack Dunlevy had trusted him to do the entire job himself.

Armpit had made sure the sprinkler heads were evenly distributed, so that the water would cover the entire lawn. He had carefully secured each connection.

The problem was that it was all just attached to itself. The pipes formed one giant rectangle, with no way for any water to enter the system.

He ended up having to work overtime, digging a new trench, cutting into the pipes, and attaching the main water line. "You don't have to pay me for the extra time it took," he told his boss. "I'm the one who screwed up."

"Unfortunately, I do," said Jack Dunlevy. "It's the law."

How could he explain it was all because a Kaira DeLeon song came on the radio?

At least he hadn't heard from Detective Newberg again. Maybe X-Ray was right. The Austin Police Department had better things to do than investigate who had sold counterfeit tickets to an African American teenager who lived on the wrong side of I-35.

He wondered if she had checked his record and found out about his prior conviction. He didn't want her to think badly of him.

Cherry Lane called once, to ask how he was doing. His mother had answered the phone and was very impressed when she realized who she was talking to.

Armpit was disappointed it wasn't Kaira.

"Why'd the mayor call you?" his mother asked him.

"Remember, I told you I met her? I did some work at her house."

For the first time in a long while, his mother looked at him and saw someone who maybe wasn't all bad.

Now it was Thursday evening, eleven days since he saw Kaira, and he was trying to get through a chapter in economics. The final exam was in eight days.

He'd thought about asking Matt Kapok if he might want to study together. They greeted each other every day in class. But he didn't want to leave the house, just in case Kaira called, and he would have been embarrassed to invite Matt over here, where, who knows, his parents might accuse Matt of being a drug dealer.

The speech final was also a week from Friday, but he wasn't too worried about that. There were no more speeches due, and the stuff in the book was all obvious stuff, like how you should look your prospective employer in the eye at a job interview.

He reread a paragraph in his econ book and studied the graph next to it. It was just beginning to make sense when the phone rang, shattering his thoughts.

He waited nervously for a moment before returning to the graph.

"Theodore, telephone!" his mother called.

He tried to remain calm. Most likely it was just X-Ray. He took a deep breath, then went into the kitchen.

His mother mouthed the words "a girl" as she handed him the phone.

"Yeah, hi," he said, trying to sound casual.

"Hi, how's it going?"

He recognized the slightly nasal voice of Detective Debbie Newberg. He walked back into his bedroom as he spoke to her.

"Oh, uh, fine."

"You probably thought I'd forgotten about you."

"Uh, no, not really."

"How certain are you that the guy's name was Habib?"

"Not real certain."

"Could it have been Felix?"

"Felix? No, I don't think so."

"How about Moses?"

"No. I'm pretty sure he said it was Habib."

"Maybe he had a nickname. Is that possible?"

"I guess."

"Did he ever refer to himself as X-Ray?"

He took a breath, then said he'd never heard that name before.

"How about Armpit?"

He almost dropped the phone.

"Hello? Are you there?"

"Yeah. Yeah, I'm here."

"Does Armpit ring a bell?"

"No, I think I would have remembered a name like that."

Debbie Newberg laughed. "I suppose so," she said.

Armpit looked at his economics book opened on his desk. He knew he could forget about studying tonight.

22

A letter came the next day. Armpit checked the mail when he got home from school. It was addressed to Theodore A. Johnson, and its return address was the Hotel del Coronado in San Diego. His middle name was Thomas.

The letter was written with a purple pen on hotel stationery in remarkably neat handwriting.

Dear T (or should I say Dear A?),

I hope you don't mind a long and dopey letter. I know it's going to be long and dopey, because every letter I've written to you has been long and dopey. They just keep getting longer and dopier! Of course, I don't actually mail them, so I guess it doesn't matter whether you mind or not.

I always say all kinds of stupid things about how much I miss you, and wish you were here, and lame junk like that. Once I even used the L word! How dumb is that??? Nobody falls in L after a bowl of ice cream and a ten-minute walk! Now you know why I didn't mail the letters. I may be dumb, but I'm not stupid!!!

It's just that you and Ginny are really my only friends. Is that pathetic or what? I don't mean you and Ginny are pathetic. I'm the one who's pathetic!

It feels good to write to you, even if I know you'll never read it. It sure beats talking to my shrink. I can see your face in my mind. Your eyes. Your smile makes me feel safe.

I'm so mad Dr. Doofus showed up when he did. That's my new name for him. He's a doctor of doofology.

I think you were going to kiss me. I know I wanted you to kiss me. I still do. Oh, so much!

God, this is even worse than yesterday's letter! You know, I almost sent it to you. I put a stamp on it and everything. There was a mail slot by the elevator. I held the letter over the slot. I'd lift one finger, then another. It was kind of like standing on the edge of a cliff, wondering what it would be like to jump.

Do you think I'm insane? Of course not, because you're not reading this.

When I sing love songs, it helps for me to picture someone in my mind. I used to just make up some imaginary boy of my dreams and sing about him. He looked nothing like you. He was much more handsome. Just kidding. Anyway, now, when I sing those songs, I picture you.

Don't get all freaked out. I'm not saying I love you. It just helps me sing the songs.

I wonder what you'd think if you actually read this.

Okay, Kaira, this is getting scary. You're not going to mail this letter. You're not! You're not! No way!!!!

Okay, I'm going to have to write something really embarrassing now. Then I can be sure I'll never mail it.

Okay, here goes.

I liked it when I touched your armpit. It made me feel all goosey inside.

Aaaah!

Oh, I miss you so much!!!!

XOXOXOX
Kaira

23

"Wow," Armpit said, then read the letter again. He imagined her holding the envelope above a mail slot, closing her eyes, and letting it go. Maybe she screamed.

He wished he knew how to get in touch with her. He looked at the back of the T-shirt. She probably was in Los Angeles now, but he had no idea what hotel she was staying at, or what TV character's name she was using.

It was too bad she didn't include her cell phone number, but why would she? She never planned to mail the letter.

The phone rang.

He grabbed it before the second ring. "Hello?"

"Theodore, good, I'm glad you're home."

It was Detective Newberg.

"We've got a suspect down at the station. I'd like you to be here while I question him."

He didn't know what to say. "I have to go to work. I only just got home from school."

"What time do you need to be there?"

"One o'clock. I don't even know the address of where I'm supposed to be."

"I can have an officer take you wherever you need to go."

"And I got to eat lunch first."

"What kind of pizza do you like?"

"*Pizza?* Uh, pepperoni."

"I'll send a patrolman to get you."

He hung up with Detective Newberg and called Raincreek. He got the address and left a message that he might be a little late, and that he wouldn't need Hernandez to give him a ride.

Less than ten minutes later a patrol car pulled into the driveway.

"Can I sit in the front seat?" Armpit asked. "I don't want my neighbors to think I'm being arrested again."

He regretted those words as soon as they escaped his mouth, but the police officer just said, "Sure, hop in." Maybe the officer hadn't heard him exactly. Or else the cops already knew about his criminal record.

The police station was a three-story stucco building. Armpit recognized the place. It was where he had been taken after the fight in the movie theater.

A sign warned that all visitors were subject to search, but he just walked through the metal detector and went with the officer up to the second floor.

Detective Newberg stepped out of a room, saw Armpit, and gave him a little wave. "Come have a look," she said, then put her finger to her lips, indicating for him to be quiet.

He went with her back into the room, which was dark and smelled like pizza. One slice had already been eaten from the box on the table.

"It's good pizza," said Debbie Newberg. Her cheeks reddened.

A window looked out into another room. The room was almost identical to his but brightly lit. X-Ray was sitting at a table, his fingers drumming nervously. Armpit could hear the tapping through the speakers on the wall.

"Is that Habib?" Detective Newberg asked quietly.

He almost laughed but then just shook his head.

"You're sure?"

"Definitely not him."

"I want you to listen while I interview him, and let me know if anything he says strikes a chord."

She gave him a pad of paper and a pen out of her briefcase in case he wanted to make notes.

She left him alone in the room, then a moment later sat down across from X-Ray. Armpit listened while she advised X-Ray that even though he was not under arrest, he still had the right to remain silent, and the right to have an attorney present during questioning.

Armpit had never known X-Ray to remain silent.

"Why would I need a lawyer?" X-Ray asked. "I'm cooperating, right? Write that down. I'm being cooperative."

Detective Newberg flashed her girlish smile, then made a note on her yellow pad.

Don't be fooled by her smile, Armpit thought, trying to telepathically send the message through the wall.

"You understand that you are not under arrest and are free to leave whenever you wish."

X-Ray nodded.

"Please answer audibly."

"Affirmative," said X-Ray.

"You also understand that this interview is being recorded."

"Affirmative," X-Ray said again.

"You also understand that although you are not under arrest, you are still a suspect in this case. Anything you say today may later be used as evidence in court."

"Affirmative," said X-Ray. He liked saying that word.

"And that you have the right not to answer any questions, and you're knowingly and freely giving up that right."

"Like I said, I want to cooperate. I got nothing to hide, right?"

"Will you state your name for the record?"

"Rex Alvin Washburn."

"And your age?"

"Seventeen."

"Do you ever go by a name other than Rex?"

"No."

"X-Ray, perhaps?" Again she smiled.

"X-Ray?" X-Ray repeated.

"Before you say something stupid, I think you should know I spoke to several people who bought concert tickets from someone who called himself X-Ray. His cell phone number is the same as yours. And we've seen the license plate on your car."

"Right, I was just about to tell you that. You have to give me a chance. You can't just ask questions without giving me a chance to explain."

"Sorry."

"See, when you asked if I had another name, I don't really think of X-Ray as another name. It's pig latin for Rex. See, like you're Debbie, right? So in pig latin that would be Ebbie-Day. It's the same name, just a different language."

"I understand," Detective Newberg reassured him. "So just to be clear, when these people told me they bought tickets from X-Ray, they really bought them from you."

"Right. My point exactly."

"How many tickets did you sell?"

X-Ray hesitated. Armpit knew what he was thinking. He was trying to figure what she knew, and if it was worth lying about.

"Twelve."

"You sure it wasn't fourteen?"

"No, just twelve."

"How much did you sell them for?"

"I charged a small service fee. It's not illegal. It's called free enterprise, protected by the Constitution."

"How much?"

"I didn't twist anybody's arm. They all came to me. They wanted the tickets, and I charged a fair price. If they didn't think it was fair, they didn't have to buy them."

"I just want to know how much."

"A hundred and thirty-five dollars."

"Did you sell any for any more than that?"

"Yeah, I sold two for three hundred."

"Three hundred each ticket, or three hundred total?"

"Each. But I had expenses, too, you know. It wasn't all profit. I had to pay for an ad in the newspaper. And gasoline's not cheap. Plus I stood in line for like six hours. Time is money, right?"

"Did you have a partner?"

"No. I'm independent."

"Ever heard of someone named Habib?"

"Habib? No."

"How about Armpit?"

X-ray didn't even flinch. "Armpit? Is that really like someone's name?"

"Apparently. So you don't know him?"

X-Ray shook his head.

"Please answer audibly."

X-Ray chuckled and said, "No, I never heard of nobody named Armpit."

"How did you first go about acquiring the tickets?"

"Say what?"

"The tickets you sold. Where did you get them? You mentioned standing in line for six hours."

"Right. I acquired them the day they went on sale."

"At the Lonestar Arena?"

"Right. I got there the night before and waited in line for like twelve hours."

"How much did you pay for the tickets?"

"Seven hundred and twenty dollars. Talk about a rip-off. They're supposed to sell for fifty-five a piece, but they charge a five-dollar service charge for each ticket."

"That doesn't seem fair," Detective Newberg agreed. "But here's something I don't get. I heard there was a limit of six tickets per customer. How did you manage to buy twelve?"

"I just did."

"I heard they were pretty strict about that."

"You're right. Okay. Here's what happened."

Keep It Simple, Stupid, thought Armpit.

"Like you said, you can only buy six tickets. Six tickets *at a time.* There's nothing that prevents someone from buying six tickets, then getting back in line and buying six more tickets."

"But it was a long line, wasn't it?"

"Yeah, it was. But you can always pay someone like fifty dollars to cut in line. See, that's another expense. That's what I'm talking about. People think ticket scalpers just make tons of money, but the expenses can really add up."

"That wasn't what I was thinking," said Detective Newberg. "You want to hear what I was thinking?"

"Go ahead."

"Thank you. I was thinking about the fact that all twelve tickets were in the same row, right next to each other. I'm wondering how you could buy six, then go back in line and buy six more, and they're all right next to each other."

"I can explain that."

"I suggest you don't," said Detective Newberg.

"But you said—"

"I don't want to hear your explanation," Detective Newberg said.

"See, I never said I went back in line. I said you *can* pay someone to cut in line, but I didn't say I—"

"Shut up and listen!"

X-Ray stopped talking.

"It's a crime to give false information to a police officer. And for someone like yourself, with a prior offense and still on probation, you could be facing quite a bit of jail time."

"You know about that?" asked X-Ray.

"You're not dealing with children here. Let me tell you what else I know. I know you went to a restaurant called Smokestack Lightnin' with somebody named Armpit. So I know you lied when you said you didn't know him. Any other lies you want to tell me?"

X-Ray didn't answer.

"You see that mirror? You're a smart guy, X-Ray. Do you think that's a regular mirror? You think it's in here so I can fix my makeup?"

"No," X-Ray answered quietly.

"No, it's a two-way mirror. Behind it is an expert criminal psychologist. He's watching and listening to everything you say. He knows when you're lying just by your body language, and by the inflection of your voice."

X-Ray gave a little wave to the "psychological expert."

Armpit waved back.

"So what I want you to do is think about everything you told me, and see if there are any corrections you might want to make."

"See, if you just let me explain—"

"Think before you talk," said Detective Newberg. "And you better tell me the truth this time, or else the DA will get this recording."

"I'm tryin' to tell you the truth, if you'll just listen. You're right, I didn't buy all the tickets myself, but it was my money! Look, let's say you're at the store, and all you want to buy is a candy bar, but there's a real long line. And then you see somebody you know at the front of the line, so you give her your dollar and she buys the candy bar for you. Then later, if someone asks you where you got the candy bar, you'll say you bought it at the store. It's not a lie, is it?"

"Who helped you buy the tickets?"

"Armpit."

"Do you know his real name?"

182

"Habib, I think."

"You think?"

"I don't know the dude! I swear! Felix called him Armpit. I never even saw the dude until that day in line. See, I went to buy my tickets, and they told me I could only buy six, like you said. So then Felix and Armpit show up, and Armpit offers to buy the other six for me. Man, that was the biggest mistake I ever made in my life."

"How do you mean?"

"You know, I thought I would just have to pay Armpit fifty bucks or something, for doing that for me. But no. He insisted I make him my partner. And let me tell you something else. Armpit is not someone you can say no to. I'm talking big, and mean, and tough. That's why I lied and said I didn't know him. If I'm going to have to testify against Armpit, then you better put me in the witness protection program."

"What was your arrangement with him?"

"We split all the profits, fifty-fifty. He was there with me for every sale."

"Do you know his last name?"

"No."

"Where does he live?"

"I have no idea."

"Do you know his phone number?"

"No."

"I'm getting tired of this, Rex."

"I swear. I'm not lying!"

"Then how would you get in touch with him?"

"I'd call Felix. Then Felix would call Armpit, and we'd meet at H-E-B."

"Who kept the tickets?"

"He kept six, I kept six. To be honest, I thought he was going to rip me off, but he never did."

Detective Newberg set her briefcase on the table and unlatched the clasps.

"Look, I'm sorry for not being totally straight with you earlier," X-Ray said. "Armpit scares the bejesus out of me. But now I told you the truth, so everything's cool, right?" He smiled. "No harm, no foul?"

Detective Newberg suddenly turned and seemed to stare right at Armpit, although he knew she couldn't see him.

She looked away, then removed two photographs from her briefcase. "Is this Felix?"

"Yeah, that's him."

She showed X-Ray a photo of Moses. "Is this Armpit?"

X-Ray took his time studying the photo. "No, Armpit's got dark skin. And he didn't wear a cowboy hat. He wore one of those things, what are they called, a turban? I think he might be part Iranian."

"Did he have a mustache?"

X-Ray thought a moment.

Armpit couldn't remember if he told X-Ray he'd said Habib had a mustache.

"He might have. The guy was so hairy it was kind of hard

to tell. He's the kind of guy who has to shave three times a day, if you know what I mean."

"How old was he?"

"Maybe twenty-five. Hard to say because of the turban."

Detective Newberg sighed. "Thank you for your cooperation," she said. She handed him her card and told him if he ever heard from Armpit again to call her.

"I can go?"

She nodded.

A uniformed officer came in and escorted X-Ray out of the room.

Armpit watched Detective Newberg place the photographs back in her briefcase. She shook her head, then walked out of the room.

A moment later the door to his room opened.

"So what does my expert criminal psychologist think?" She smiled, and her cheeks turned pink.

"I think he told the truth."

"You're kidding, right?"

"I mean, not at first, but then you scared him and I think he told you the truth after that."

Detective Newberg shook her head. "Now I understand how Armpit managed to sell you those phony tickets. You are way too gullible."

Armpit shrugged.

She smiled. "It's because you're honest. Oh, you didn't eat your pizza."

He'd lost his appetite.

"Well, even if X-Ray won't tell us how to find Habib, it shouldn't be all that hard to find someone whose name is Armpit. We could probably smell him a mile away."

She laughed at her own joke.

"He didn't smell bad to me," Armpit said. "I mean, that might have nothing to do with his name. Maybe a wasp stung him on the armpit or something like that."

He just had to get that in.

24

It had never felt so good to be digging and sweating in the hot sun. He didn't have to think about anything except dirt and shrubs.

Detective Newberg ended up driving him to work, which was just as well since she drove a normal car and he didn't have to explain about showing up in a black-and-white. He did his best to back up what X-Ray had said. He confirmed that Habib wore a turban.

X-Ray called him later and told him he'd had a nice chat with Debbie Newberg and that everything was cool now, but just in case, it might be a good idea if they stayed away from each other for a while.

Armpit didn't have the heart to tell him he'd seen and

heard the whole thing. Instead, he told X-Ray about Kaira's letter.

"You dog! If you end up marrying that chick, you owe me at least a half a million dollars."

The phone rang the second he hung up with X-Ray.

"Okay, I just want to warn you that you're going to get a really, really dumb letter, so don't read it. Don't even open the envelope. Just take a match to it."

When he told her he'd already read it, Kaira screamed so loud he had to hold the phone away from his ear.

Then she complained about the unreliability of the U.S. Postal Service. "I thought they were supposed to be *slow*! You must think I'm a total lamebrain."

"I liked the letter."

"You did?"

"I liked it a lot. It made me feel good inside. Not all goosey, kind of ducklike."

"What?"

"Nothing. I was just trying to make a joke."

"So what do all your friends think about you having a famous rock star for a girlfriend?"

He didn't know she was his girlfriend, but he was glad she thought she was.

"I haven't really told anyone."

"You are so . . . I don't know. Other guys would be all braggy about it. You're just so real. So down-to-earth. I feel like a big phony whenever I talk to you."

"I don't think you're phony."

Kaira forced a laugh. "That's because you don't know me. I'm so fake I can't even tell when I'm being honest or not. Like you know when I told you to burn the letter? I was lying. I was hoping you'd read it. I just didn't want you to know I wanted that."

"I figured as much."

"You did?"

"Well, I mean, if you really wanted me to burn the letter you wouldn't have waited a few days to call me."

"You are so smart. You see right through me."

That might have been the first time anyone had ever told him he was smart.

"Okay," Kaira said, "you've got to tell me something embarrassing about you now."

"Why?"

"Because I wrote an embarrassing letter to you."

"I didn't ask you to write it."

"You have to," said Kaira. "That way we'll be even. Otherwise I'll never be able to look at you again."

"All right," Armpit agreed. He thought a moment. "All right, you know that song 'Damsel in Distress'?"

"Uh, yeah, I think I've heard of it," Kaira said sarcastically.

"Well, yeah, I know you know the song. What are the words after 'this something, this something, this dress. You would never guess . . .'—then what comes next?"

"Why?"

"Because every time I hear the song it sounds like you're singing something, but I know it can't be that."

"What does it sound like?"

"Okay, this is really embarrassing, but you asked for it. Every time I hear the song, it sounds like you're singing, 'Armpit. Save me, Armpit. A damsel in distress.' "

Kaira laughed. " 'Save me, Armpit'!" she exclaimed. "Why would I sing 'Save me, Armpit'? That doesn't make sense."

"I know!"

"I didn't even know that was your name! I didn't even know you when I recorded the song!"

"I know! I know you weren't really singing that. I already told you that."

"God, you're even worse than me. I just wrote you a dumb letter. You're delusional!"

"So are you going to tell me the real words or not?"

"I didn't know there was anybody in the world named Armpit!"

"Will you humor me and tell me the words?"

Kaira recited the words. " 'These shoes, these jewels, this dress. A perfect picture of success. You would never guess . . .' " She paused and said the next two words slowly and clearly. " '*I'm but* a damsel in distress. Save me. I'm but a damsel in distress.' "

"Well, that makes more sense," Armpit agreed.

"You are so funny," said Kaira. "Just hearing your voice. You don't know how much I miss you."

"Me too."

"Really?"

"Yeah, I really do. I tried not to miss you too much, because I never thought I'd ever hear from you again, but once I got your letter, and now hearing you . . . It's like your voice cuts right to my heart."

"Aw, you are so sweet. You know what we should do? We're going to be staying in San Francisco for three days this weekend. I'll be doing a show there, a show in Marin, and one in Berkeley. You should come visit me!"

"Yeah, right, I'll just hop on my private jet."

"We fly people in all the time. A guitar player gets sick or something."

"You're serious."

"I am serious. We'll arrange everything. A limo will pick you up at your house and take you to the airport."

"You're serious?"

"Three days in San Francisco. Just you and me. What do you say?"

It was incomprehensible to him. She might as well have asked him if he wanted to fly to the moon. Which was probably why he said what he said.

"Sure, why not?"

25

"You have to t-tell your p-parents," said Ginny.

"Why?"

"Because. They're your parents."

They were taking their daily walk.

"Think about it, Ginny," said Armpit. "Do you really think I'm going to San Francisco? Look around. Do you really think a limo is going to come driving up this street and park in our driveway?"

"Yes."

Armpit stared off in the distance. "San Franciso," he said.

"San Francisco," Ginny repeated.

"I'm scared of earthquakes," he told her.

◆　◆　◆

A woman named Aileen called him on Tuesday and asked him for his United Airlines frequent flyer number. When he told her he didn't have one, she said United was the only airline that flew nonstop from Austin to San Francisco, and she suggested he enroll in their frequent flyer program when he got to the airport since he'd be getting double miles for flying first class.

She sounded incredibly efficient. She rattled off several departure and arrival times as he struggled to keep up. She suggested he take the 11:55 flight, which got into San Franciso at 1:10, because the only other nonstop would get him in at 6:21, which might make it difficult to make the eight o'clock show in Berkeley, depending on traffic, unless he wanted to fly into Oakland, in which case he would fly American, but there would be a layover in Dallas.

He went with her first suggestion.

"The eleven-fifty-five?"

"Whatever you said."

It wasn't until after he hung up that it occurred to him he'd miss his economics final. That was, if he really went.

Aileen sat at an antique desk looking over the hills of Santa Barbara and out to the Pacific Ocean. Unfortunately, what the hotel offered in charm and serenity, it lacked in modern technology, such as in-room Internet connections. She'd had to connect her laptop to her cell phone but kept losing reception. Which meant she still hadn't booked Theodore Johnson's ticket.

She heard the click of her door being unlocked, and then Jerome Paisley poked his large head into the room. "Have you made the arrangements?"

She lazily glanced his way. "I just have to book the flight."

"Wait till you hear this?" he said, coming up behind her. "You won't believe it!"

"Tell me."

Jerome massaged the back of her neck as he spoke. "Fred ran a background check. The kid's got a criminal record. Assault and battery!"

Aileen turned around to look at him.

"Am I a genius or am I a genius?"

She rose from her chair, then stood on tiptoe to kiss him. "You're a genius," she whispered.

"See, genius isn't all about *intelligence*," he explained. "There are a lot of smart people in the world. Smarter than me. It's about *recognizing your opportunities*. It's about letting your opportunities come to you. Sometimes all you have to do is open the door and opportunity walks right in. It takes a genius to know when to open the door."

Aileen knew a thing or two herself about recognizing opportunities. She had recognized Jerome Paisley as a weak, insecure man who was constantly trying to impress everybody. She let herself be impressed.

So far, with the help of Jerome, she had managed to extract nearly three million dollars from Kaira's trust account. Even he didn't know the extent of her embezzlement.

Jerome began to pace. "Now's the time. Now's the time,"

he said, talking more to himself than to Aileen. "She'll be eighteen in two months. Now's the time to act. Opportunity is knocking. I've got no choice. Now's the time to open the door."

He was rambling. Aileen could hear the fear in his voice. She could see it in his eyes.

Kaira had said many times that she planned to fire him when she turned eighteen. If that happened, then whoever took his place would certainly discover the embezzlement. However, if, for example, somebody like Billy Boy killed Kaira before she turned eighteen, then her mother would inherit all her money. Jerome, her mother's husband, would continue to oversee all the financial matters.

"She's not a golden goose!" he declared. "I'm the golden goose. She'd still be singing in her church choir if it weren't for me. I made her who she is, and I can find someone else just as easily."

His plan was to stay with Kaira's mother for a couple of years to avoid suspicion, then divorce her and live with Aileen. But those weren't Aileen's plans. She had no intention of sharing her money or her life with that self-absorbed maniac.

Which was why in addition to needing to book a ticket for Theodore Johnson, she planned to book one for herself: first to Portland, then to Costa Rica. The name on her passport was Denise Linaria.

One thing for certain. She did not want to be anywhere near San Francisco when Theodore Johnson got there.

◆ ◆ ◆

The concert that night was in an outside amphitheater, nestled in the foothills. Kaira waited on a patio offstage. The ocean air was cool and foggy. She could smell the flowers that bloomed around the Santa Barbara Mission.

She couldn't believe she'd be seeing Theodore again in just three days. Aileen had booked the ticket. It almost made her like Aileen again.

More than once she had thought about telling her mother about Aileen, but she couldn't bring herself to do it. It wasn't just that she didn't want to hurt her mother. As much as she hated to admit it, the sad truth was that she, Kaira, *needed* El Genius. Despite all her bluster, deep down she knew there was no way she would ever fire him. She'd be lost without him.

Once the concert started she was able to shut out all thoughts about her mother and El Genius and just disappear into the music. Out in the open air, her voice seemed to float all the way up to the stars. And nobody noticed, not the band, not the audience, when this time she really did sing:

"Save me, Armpit!
A damsel in distress."

26

Uncharacteristically, Jack Dunlevy wore a jacket and tie. Armpit told him he looked sharp, but Jack just grumbled something about not having enough neck room. He had to go to some kind of meeting at the mayor's office.

They were at a house where two months earlier they'd installed a sprinkler system. Now there was a leak. "It's somewhere on the right side of the front yard," his boss told him.

"My right, or the house's right?" Armpit asked.

"What?"

"I mean, is it on the right when I'm standing in the street facing the house, or when I'm standing at the front door facing the street?"

"Just find the damn leak and fix it!"

He was edgy about the meeting and his clothes made him uncomfortable. Plus the homeowner wouldn't be paying him for this, no matter what caused the leak, but he still had to pay Armpit.

He left for his meeting, and Armpit looked over the area. There was no easy way to find a leak. He would just have to dig along every inch of pipe.

And he was just about to do that when a mountain laurel planted near the corner of the house caught his attention. He hadn't remembered that mountain laurel being there the last time.

He realized, of course, that he'd worked at forty houses, at least, and couldn't remember every plant in every yard. Still, he had to start digging somewhere, so he started there.

It took him less than twenty minutes to find the leak. Whoever had planted the mountain laurel had cut a gash into the sprinkler line with a shovel.

He sawed off a two-foot section of the damaged pipe, then attached a new piece. He had to let the glue dry before he could test it, so he was sitting in the shade when a car pulled up.

He assumed it was someone coming to see the homeowner, so it took a moment for his brain to register that the guy getting out of the driver's seat was Felix and the guy in the cowboy hat was Moses.

Moses pulled a third person out of the back seat—X-Ray. X-Ray had a large bruise on his right cheek, and he wasn't wearing his glasses. His shirt was ripped.

Armpit rose to his feet. "Are you all right? What's going on?"

"Everything's cool," X-Ray said as Moses shoved him along. "They just want to talk to you."

There was something wrong with X-Ray's mouth, and he spoke with a little bit of a lisp.

"Where are his glasses?" Armpit asked.

Moses pulled X-Ray's glasses out of his front shirt pocket, held them a moment, then dropped them on the lawn.

"Have you heard?" asked Felix. "Somebody's been selling counterfeit tickets. This lady cop came to talk to me about it. To me! I never sold a phony ticket in my life. I explain it's bad for business. Sure, I might make a quick buck, but then I'd never sell another ticket. See, my business is based on trust."

"I told you. She doesn't think it was you," said X-Ray.

Moses whacked him on the side of his head. "And I told you to shut up," he said in his unusually high voice.

"Have you read the newspapers lately?" asked Felix. "The mayor's all charged up. Got to stop all the counterfeit ticket sales! What do you think that does to my business?"

"People trust you, Felix," said X-Ray. "You're known all around town. Every hotel concierge and—"

"Shut up!" said Moses.

Felix continued. "Now they're even talking about passing a law to make ticket scalping illegal."

"They can't do that," X-Ray said. "It's unconstitutional."

Moses whacked him again. "Man, what does it take?" He turned back to Armpit. "How do you put up with him?"

"You know what the cop asks me?" Felix asked. "You want to know her number-one question? 'Where's Armpit?' That's her question. 'Where does he live? What's his phone number?' And all I'm thinking is: *Who the hell is Armpit?* But then it comes to me. I remember those two dudes I met at the Lonestar. I kinda liked those guys. They seemed cool. So I tell her I never heard of nobody named Armpit."

"We appreciate that," said X-Ray.

"Shut up!"

"But you know what happens when there's a loss of trust? People are afraid to buy tickets. Demand goes down. Prices drop. Way I figure it, Armpit, your two little phony tickets have cost me about two thousand dollars so far."

"Armpit didn't know anything about it!" said X-Ray.

Moses was about to hit X-Ray again, but Armpit took a step toward him. "Don't touch him."

"Oh, yeah?" said Moses, challenging him. "What are you going to do about it?"

"Settle down," said Felix. "Here's the thing, Armpit. I could tell Detective Cutie-pie everything I know, but how does that help me?"

"It doesn't," said X-Ray.

"It doesn't," Felix agreed. "The damage is already done. But maybe there's a way we could help each other. You help me make my money back, and even make some money for yourself while you're at it."

"What do you have in mind?" Armpit asked, his eyes on Moses.

"Kaira DeLeon's letter. I'll pay you a hundred and fifty dollars for it."

"It's not for sale," Armpit said firmly as he shot a glance at X-Ray.

Felix smiled. He turned to Moses. "What do you know? Our friend X-Ray wasn't lying."

"Hey, I've never lied to you," X-Ray said. "You just got to understand where I'm coming from."

A pickup truck pulled up behind Felix's car.

"Look, here's the deal, Armpit. You sell me the letter or else I talk to Detective Cutie-pie. Your choice. Everybody wins, or everybody loses."

Jack Dunlevy got out of the truck. He no longer wore his jacket and tie.

"You got twenty-four hours," Felix said, then handed Armpit a business card with his phone number on it. "By the way, is your real name Habib?"

Armpit didn't answer.

The heel of Moses's boot came down on X-Ray's glasses; then he and Felix headed back to their car, crossing paths with Jack Dunlevy coming the other way.

"Sorry, man," X-Ray said. "I'm really sorry. The only reason I told him about the letter was because I was trying to explain how no one got hurt by the phony tickets."

"Yeah, well, sometimes you talk too much," said Armpit.

"I do," X-Ray agreed. "I do talk too much."

Armpit picked up X-Ray's glasses. The frames were bent and a lens had popped out, but there was nothing that couldn't be fixed.

"Well, you just do what you think is right," X-Ray said. "Don't worry about me. If I go to jail, it's my own fault."

Jack Dunlevy came toward them. "I'm not paying you to stand around and talk to your friends," he said, but didn't sound especially angry.

"I fixed the leak," Armpit told him. "I was just waiting for it to dry so I could test it."

His boss looked around at the relatively undisturbed lawn.

Armpit told him about the mountain laurel.

His boss smiled, then turned to X-Ray. "See, that's why I'm giving him a raise and a promotion. He's got more than a strong back. He's got a brain, too."

The meeting had been a success. Jack Dunlevy told Armpit he got the contract to landscape the performing arts center. He was going to have to hire a whole bunch of new people. And he wasn't kidding about the raise and promotion. "You'll have your own crew. We start this weekend."

He turned back to X-Ray. "So what happened to you? Was it those guys?"

"I'm okay."

"You wouldn't like a job, would you? Six-fifty an hour?"

"Sounds good," X-Ray said, much to Armpit's surprise. "But I want to be up-front with you straight off. I've got a record."

Jack Dunlevy considered a moment. "You at Green Lake too?" he asked.

"Yes, sir. That's where I met Theodore."

Armpit almost laughed. It sounded strange to hear X-Ray call him by his real name.

"In that case I'll make it seven dollars an hour," said Armpit's boss. "You guys are the fastest diggers."

27

Armpit's economics teacher once told the class about a donkey standing exactly halfway between two identical haystacks. Since it had no reason to choose one haystack over the other, it just stayed in the middle until it died of hunger.

Everyone in the class argued that a donkey wouldn't really do that, but that wasn't the point. Actually, Armpit couldn't remember what the point was. Like a lot of what he learned in economics, it didn't make sense in the real world.

But the image of that donkey remained in his head all year. He couldn't get rid of it. Its long ears drooped and its head hung low as it became thinner and thinner. He wanted to scream at it. "Just pick one and go eat!"

Now he was beginning to understand what it felt like to be that donkey.

He didn't study for his economics test. He didn't call Felix. He didn't tell his parents about Kaira DeLeon inviting him to San Francisco. He didn't tell his boss that he couldn't work this weekend.

Armpit figured that Felix would probably sell the letter on eBay. He'd heard about a piece of gum chewed by Madonna going for six thousand dollars.

Just what Kaira wanted—her personal letter read by millions of people over the Internet. But if he didn't sell Felix the letter, then X-Ray would go to jail. Maybe he would too. If he went to San Francisco he'd fail economics.

And so he remained, paralyzed by indecision, a donkey between two haystacks.

28

He lay awake all Thursday night, but when he got out of bed Friday morning he had a plan. It didn't solve all his problems, but at least he'd come to a decision. He realized he couldn't do everything. He couldn't please everybody.

He called Felix, then went to school and took his speech final. It was ridiculously easy, as he knew it would be, with only multiple choice and true/false questions.

He didn't go to economics. There was no point. He hadn't read the last three chapters.

His feeling of regret was so strong that he actually felt pain walking away from the school building, but he'd made a decision and he knew he had to stick to it. He felt bad about letting Jack Dunlevy down too. Other people complained about their bosses, but Jack had been more than fair with him.

But when someone like Kaira DeLeon invited you to San Francisco, how could you not go? He could hear her voice singing in his head.

> Got no rearview mirror
> And none on either side.
> Ain't no lookin' back, babe,
> When I take you for a ride!

Who knew, he might never have to work again. Whether or not he graduated from high school wouldn't mean a whole heck of a lot.

A horn honked. He turned as the car made a sudden U-turn, then came right at him. It stopped against the curb, with its back end sticking out at a forty-five-degree angle.

Felix and Moses came out from either side.

"I want the letter now," said Felix.

"I told you Monday."

"I know what you told me. I want it today. I don't appreciate being strung along."

"I'm not stringing you along. Look, it's like you said. You talk to the police, everybody loses. You wait till Monday, everybody wins."

Moses's fist slammed against the side of Armpit's head, spinning him backward.

Armpit managed to keep from falling. He raised his hands with his palms out. "Just wait."

Moses didn't want to wait. He came at Armpit again, but this time Armpit saw him coming. Armpit ducked under the swinging fist, then charged like a bull headfirst into him.

Moses's cowboy hat flew off as he fell back against Felix's car, cracking a headlight.

He was lucky it was the headlight and not his head.

Moses got back to his feet, rubbed his hands together, and smiled at Armpit.

Armpit readied himself.

Moses took one step toward him, faked with his right, then slammed his left fist into Armpit's gut.

Armpit doubled over but fended off the next blow, and the two of them fell to the ground and rolled into the gutter, fists flying as they traded punches. Armpit took several blows to the head, but Moses's punches only got weaker, while his own seemed to gain power.

A horn sounded from the street, and Armpit looked up to see a long white limousine stopped in the middle of the road. "I called the police!" the driver shouted, pointing to his cell phone.

Armpit rose to his feet. He took a couple of steps backward as he watched the limo drive down the street and turn the corner.

"Just give me till Monday," he said. "You'll get the letter."

Moses pulled himself to his feet using the side mirror for support.

The cowboy hat lay on the ground, white with a brown band. Armpit, remembering X-Ray's glasses, stepped on it.

He walked the rest of the way home without once looking back over his shoulder.

The white limo was now parked in front of his house. The driver stood beside it, but when he saw Armpit, he got back inside and locked the doors.

Armpit knocked on the window.

The driver showed him the cell phone and started pushing the buttons.

"It's me! Theodore Johnson. I'm the guy you're here for. Just let me get my stuff."

He hurried into the house, unsure if the driver would still be there when he returned. When he saw himself in the mirror he was even more doubtful. He looked like a wild man. Sweat and blood dripped from his face onto his torn clothes. Even he would cross to the other side of the street if he saw himself coming.

There was no time to shower. He took off his shirt and splashed his face and upper body with cold water, then sprayed himself with Sploosh. A knuckle on his right hand was bleeding, so he put a Band-Aid on it.

He put on a clean shirt and put three others in his backpack, along with a pair of long pants and some socks and underwear.

In the bottom of his sock drawer was Kaira's letter and the money from the ticket sales, almost a thousand dollars. He took it all, including the letter.

He went into the kitchen, and, looking out the window, he was a little surprised to see the limo still parked out front. He wrote a note on the pad next to the telephone.

Dear Mom and Dad,
*   I won't be back until Sunday night. It's just something*
I got to do. Don't worry.

T

He didn't know what else he could say. He realized he should call Jack Dunlevy, but there wasn't time and he didn't know what he'd say to him, either. He just had to hope that X-Ray would cover for him. He grabbed his back-pack and went outside.

The limousine driver came around and opened the door for him. "Welcome, Mr. Johnson," he said. "Sorry I didn't realize who you were before."

"I'm just glad you're still here," Armpit said, settling into the backseat.

"There's water and a newspaper," the driver pointed out.

"Thanks."

The *Austin American Statesman* lay on the seat next to him, and there were two bottles of water in side cup holders. Armpit finished the first bottle before the car made it onto the highway.

In the panel above him were the radio and temperature controls. Armpit studied the knobs, then turned the air conditioner to MAX.

"I've got an envelope for you with your travel documents," the driver told him. "Apparently your fax machine wasn't working."

Armpit smiled.

Kaira's voice came over the radio.

> A sad circus clown who has hopes to inspire
> The love of the long-haired, blue-spangled trapeze
>   highflyer,
> Kicks off his floppy shoes and changes attire,
> Just like Clark Kent, or Tobey Maguire,
> And goes up the circus ladder, higher and higher,
> 'Cause a clown is someone she could never
>   admire,
> But there ain't no net beneath the high wire.
> Nearing the top, he starts to perspire.
> He's climbing out of the frying pan . . .
> And into the fire!

29

There was a long line at the ticket counter, but Armpit breezed right past it and went to the one for first-class passengers, where there was almost no wait. The ticket agent called him Mr. Johnson.

He went through security without being searched, which surprised him because they stopped a middle-aged bald guy with glasses. Even Armpit knew he looked more dangerous than that guy did.

A couple of hours later he was flying over the Rocky Mountains and eating a caramel sundae. The man beside him lived in San Francisco.

"You ever been in an earthquake?" Armpit asked.

"Lots of times. Nothing to worry about. You just duck

under a desk or stand in a doorway until the shaking stops."

Armpit had an image of himself cowering under a desk with plaster and bricks crashing around him, and big gaps in the floor opening on all sides.

The plane landed ten minutes early, at exactly one o'clock Pacific daylight time. Armpit took the escalator down to the baggage claim, where he spotted a man holding a sign with THEODORE JOHNSON on it. The man had a baggage cart, but Armpit told him that all he had was his backpack, which he carried himself to the limo.

It was hot and sunny at the airport, although nothing like the oppressive heat of Texas, but when he arrived at the Wellington Arms Hotel in downtown San Francisco twenty-five minutes later, fog had filled the air and the temperature was downright cold. It was hard to believe this was the middle of July. He wished he'd brought a jacket.

Ginny will never believe it, he thought as he took a breath of ocean air. It was like the whole city was air-conditioned. There was also a freshness to the air that he didn't get in Texas, where it seemed that the same hot and humid air stayed in one place all summer long, becoming more stale and stagnant by the minute.

A doorman asked if he needed help with his luggage, but Armpit told him no thanks, showing that his backpack was all he had.

When he walked through the revolving door, it seemed like he had stepped into a palace. Once again he thought of Ginny. He wished she could see this. "Grand" and "spectacular." Those were the words he'd use when telling her about it. All around were giant chandeliers and ornate mirrors. "Ornate." That was another word he'd use.

A thin, attractive Asian woman wearing a blue pantsuit approached him. "Mr. Johnson?"

"Yeah, that's me." She was the fourth person to call him Mr. Johnson that day.

"It's a pleasure to have you with us. I'm Nancy Young."

He shook her hand. A brass name tag attached to her blazer had her name and the words VIP GUEST RELATIONS.

"Let me know if there's anything you need." She gave him an envelope with the keys to his room and minibar. "You're on the twenty-first floor. Everything's already been taken care of. Do you need a bellman?"

"No, I just have my backpack is all."

She explained that he was on a restricted floor and would need to use his room key in the elevator. "Would you like me to show you how that works?"

"No, that's all right." He thought about asking her what he should do in case of an earthquake but didn't want to sound like a wimp. The twenty-first floor was pretty high up. It didn't seem like ducking under a desk would do much good if the whole building fell over.

He looked around for the elevators, then started off in

the wrong direction, but Nancy Young stopped him. "The elevators are right over there," she said.

Now that he saw them, he wondered how he had missed them in the first place. They were right out in the open. "Sorry, I've never been in this hotel before."

"Yes, it can be quite confusing," she said without even a hint of sarcasm in her voice.

She walked with him to the elevator, then showed him how to insert his room key card into the slot to gain access to the twenty-first floor.

"Enjoy your stay."

His hotel room turned out to be a two-room suite. A fruit and cheese plate had been left for him on a coffee table in his sitting area, compliments of the hotel. He cut off a slice of very hard cheese and put it on a cracker. It tasted bitter, but he figured it was supposed to taste that way. He popped a couple of red grapes into his mouth.

There were two television sets, one in each room, and he counted five telephones: two in each room and one in the bathroom. "Now, that's class," he said aloud when he saw the one in the bathroom, easily reachable from the toilet.

He was taking a shower, his hair full of jasmine-avocado shampoo, when the phone rang. No problem. He opened the shower door and reached for the phone.

"Hello."

"You're here! Why didn't you call me?"

"I'm just getting cleaned up."

"Well, hurry. I've been waiting all day! God, I can't be-lieve you're really here. I can't wait to see you. I'm going out of my mind!"

"Me too."

"Call me as soon as you're ready. I'm in room 2122. My name's Lisa Simpson."

He rinsed the soap out of his hair, brushed his teeth, and used the complimentary mouthwash to get rid of the cheese taste. He put on long pants for the first time in nearly two months, then called Lisa Simpson, who said she'd meet him in the lobby.

He was on his way to the elevator when Kaira's business manager stopped him. "Welcome, you must be Theodore."

"Yes, sir."

Armpit had seen him twice before: first at the concert, then in the lobby of the Four Seasons.

"Jerome Paisley, Kaira's father." He extended his hand.

Armpit remembered Kaira saying something about him being married to her mother, but she never referred to him as her father. He shook the man's hand.

"Your flight okay?"

"Yeah, it was great," Armpit said. "Thanks. I really ap-preciate you bringing me out here and everything."

The man smiled. "Happy to do it. If there's anything you need, you just let me know."

"I'm fine. Everything's really great. Thanks."

"You like baseball?"

The question caught Armpit by surprise. "I guess."

"C'mon, I want to show you something."

Armpit had no choice then but to go with Kaira's manager. He didn't want to be rude.

Jerome Paisley opened the door to his hotel room. "I'll just open the door. You walk right in," he said.

It was a strange thing to say, and he said it in a strange way, but Armpit went inside.

The suite was identical to Armpit's. Kaira's stepfather slid open a closet door and pulled out a baseball bat, holding it by fat end. "Take a look at this baby!"

Armpit took the bat. "Cool." He didn't know what else to say.

"See the initials, B.B.?"

The letters were above the label.

"Barry Bonds," said Kaira's father. "Go on, take a few swings."

"That's okay," said Armpit.

"Go on, you won't break it."

Armpit took the bat, made sure he had room, then took a half swing. He felt silly.

"Feels pretty good, doesn't it?" said Jerome Paisley. "You could hit a lot of home runs with that baby."

Armpit didn't know all that much about baseball, but he was pretty sure that it wasn't the bat that hit the home runs, but the person who swung it.

"You know, I used to play pro ball," Kaira's manager told him. "Just one season in the big leagues before an injury ended my career."

One season was an exaggeration. Jerome Paisley played in the major leagues for just eighteen days in September, when teams are allowed to expand their rosters. The so-called injury was more mental than physical. After having been hit in the face by a pitch, he couldn't swing a bat without closing his eyes.

Armpit set the bat down.

"But it all worked out in the end, didn't it? Look at me now. Making more money than most ballplayers. And how long does a ballplayer's career last? Ten years if he's lucky. I'm a lot better off than they are, am I not?"

It took a second before Armpit realized that Jerome Paisley was expecting an answer. "Yes, sir, you're doing great," he said. "Look, I got to go. I'm supposed to meet Kaira downstairs."

"Hey, have fun. Don't mean to hold you up."

"Thanks. Thanks for showing me the bat." He backed out of the suite, then hurried down the hall.

Well, that was weird, he thought as he rode the elevator down to the lobby.

Kaira was waiting just outside the elevator. "It's not nice to keep a girl waiting," she said. She was all in flannel and denim, like a lumberjack.

Fred was standing a few steps away from her, but this

218

time Armpit didn't let that stop him. He went right to Kaira, grabbed her, and kissed her on the lips.

She returned the kiss, letting it linger for several seconds. Then they smiled at each other.

"I guess it was worth the wait," she whispered.

30

"You're going to freeze. I can't believe you didn't bring a jacket!" She held both his hands.

"It's summer. It's like a hundred degrees in Texas."

"You're not in Texas. You're here, with me."

"Well, you're pretty hot too," said Armpit.

She rolled her eyes but smiled. "Come on, we'll get you a sweatshirt or something at the gift shop."

She let go of one of his hands but still held the other as she led him into the boutique.

He began looking through the sweatshirts, trying to find one that wasn't too cutesy, but Kaira went straight to a charcoal gray wool jacket hanging on display.

"You'd look great in this!"

It was pretty sharp. Armpit felt the fabric, which was as

soft as Kaira's flannel shirt. He was about to try it on when he saw the price. Nine hundred and ninety-five dollars.

He returned to the sweatshirts even though Kaira told him not to worry about the price. "You just charge it to your room. The tour will pay for it."

Armpit picked out a hooded red sweatshirt that said SAN FRANCISCO on it and had a picture of a cable car. It cost a hundred and twenty dollars, but that seemed like a bargain compared to the jacket. He charged it to his room.

Kaira called him Little Red Riding Hood when he put the hood up, so he put it back down. "You want to take a walk across the Golden Gate Bridge?" she asked.

"Sounds good."

The doorman whistled for a taxi, and Kaira asked the driver if he knew the way to the Golden Gate Bridge.

"Never heard of it," the driver said, then winked at Armpit.

Armpit got in the backseat, and Kaira snuggled up next to him. "You take your own cab," she told Fred.

She felt soft and cuddly, like one of Ginny's stuffed animals.

As they pulled away from the hotel, Kaira asked Armpit for a fifty-dollar bill.

Apparently she was used to being around people who carried that kind of money. For once in his life Armpit actually had several fifties in his wallet.

"Okay, here's the deal," she told the driver, handing him Armpit's fifty. "The guy following us is a total doofus. As soon as you can ditch him, let us out, then keep on going to the bridge."

"I like your style," the driver told her.

"Me too," said Armpit.

Kaira sang, *"I like your style/and the way you smile/just drives me wild."*

Armpit didn't know if it was a real song or if she just made it up on the spot.

"You know, you got a really nice voice," the driver remarked.

The cab suddenly swerved across three lanes of traffic. Kaira laughed as she fell across Armpit's lap.

The driver told them to get ready. He turned a corner, then eased to a stop in front of a double-parked UPS truck.

"Go!"

Kaira opened the door and jumped out. Armpit only had one foot on the pavement when the driver hit the gas. He swung the door shut and grabbed Kaira's hand to keep from falling.

They crouched down behind the large brown truck as the taxi with Fred in it drove right on by.

Jerome Paisley slipped the key card into the slot and was pleased to see the green light come on. He checked the hallway one last time, then opened the door to Armpit's suite and stepped quickly inside.

He wore a pair of latex gloves, the kind worn by surgeons. They fit tight, like an extra layer of skin.

He took a quick look around the sitting area, then went into the bedroom, where Armpit's clothes were strewn across the floor. He picked up a sweat-soaked sock, considered it a moment, then let it drop.

He entered the bathroom. Armpit's wet towel lay in a heap on the floor, next to the terry-cloth bathrobe the hotel had provided. The cap was off a tube of toothpaste, and some toothpaste had leaked out. A hairbrush lay next to the mirror.

He picked up the hairbrush and removed a couple of strands of hair that were stuck to the bristles. He placed them in a plain white envelope.

A used Band-Aid, crusted with blood, lay on the floor next to the wastebasket. He picked it up, smiled at his fat face in the mirror, then placed the Band-Aid in the envelope as well.

He returned to the sitting area. Aileen was the one who had provided him with the extra key to Armpit's room. She also had given him two keys to Kaira's. He now placed one of them between the cushions on the couch.

Before leaving, he took the knife from the fruit and cheese plate.

They found themselves walking through Chinatown, his arm around her shoulders, hers around his waist. Racks of fruits and vegetables had been set out in front of small grocery stores, further blocking the already crowded sidewalks. Trucks were double-parked up and down the street. Traffic was at a standstill, and people moved in and out between the cars. Yet when Armpit and Kaira stopped and kissed by the pagoda on Grant Avenue, it seemed to each of them like they were the only two people on the street.

They continued walking. Armpit was amazed by all the people and wondered what their lives were like. He felt like he was in a foreign country. Women grumbled in Chinese as they picked through vegetables and melons that he'd never seen before.

"Look at those," he said, pointing at green beans that were well over a foot long.

"I don't like veggies," said Kaira.

The insides of the stores seemed even more exotic and mysterious than the vegetables displayed on the sidewalk, but he couldn't get her to go in one with him. She had been grossed out by a string of dead ducks hanging in a window.

"I think it's cool," said Armpit.

"That's because you're not a duck," said Kaira.

She agreed to stop at a store selling Chinese souvenirs because he wanted to buy something for Ginny. The silk slippers would have been perfect, but he didn't know what size to get, and Kaira pointed out that slippers weren't like T-shirts; they had to be an exact fit.

Going through a rack of clothes, he came across a sweatshirt that was identical to the one he was wearing. The price was nineteen ninety-nine.

"It's not the same," said Kaira. "It doesn't have a hood."

"That's one expensive hood," said Armpit.

"That's not the only difference," said Kaira. "Feel the fabric."

It didn't feel all that different to Armpit, but he didn't say so.

He ended up buying Ginny a silk scarf that showed the Golden Gate Bridge stretching across a background of blue sky and green ocean.

31

"God, I can breathe again," Kaira said. The crowds of people and the strong smells of Chinatown had gotten to her. "I could kill for a cup of coffee."

He believed her.

They were now in the Italian section of the city, which Kaira said was called North Beach, but he didn't see any sand or water. The streets were lined with Italian restaurants, cafés, bookstores, and other small shops. One shop sold nothing but old postcards.

"It's not a beach," Kaira explained. "It's just called that."

"Kind of like Camp Green Lake," said Armpit.

They went down into a basement coffeehouse. Interspersed between the tables, vertical wooden beams supported the ceiling. The wood seemed especially dark and rich, as if it had been absorbing coffee for the last fifty years.

The girl behind the counter had a teardrop tattoo under her left eye. Kaira ordered a double cappuccino and asked for whipped cream on top.

"The same," said Armpit. He would have felt dumb asking for a Coke in a place like this.

The coffee was served in cups the size of soup bowls. The eternally crying girl sprinkled powdered chocolate over the whipped cream. Kaira picked out some kind of twisted pastry that was big enough for them to share, then took her coffee and pastry and went looking for a table.

"Nine dollars and twenty cents," said the girl behind the counter.

Armpit was surprised by how cheerful she sounded. He paid with a ten and left the change in the tip jar.

Kaira was emptying a packet of sugar into her coffee when he sat down next to her. The remains of another sugar packet lay in a small coffee puddle next to her cup.

"Isn't this place great?" she asked. "Beatniks used to read poetry and play bongos on that stage."

The stage was a triangular space in the corner, raised about a foot off the floor. It was empty now, but there were small posters attached to the beams, advertising various folksingers and poets who would be performing over the next few weeks.

Armpit just hoped the beams were strong enough to

hold up in an earthquake. If they'd been around since beat-
nik times, they must be strong, he thought. Either that or
they were ready to break at the next little shake.

He tried to take a sip of his cappuccino but couldn't
quite figure out how to do it without getting whipped cream
on his nose.

"I'd like to sing on a small stage like that. No flashing
lights. No backup singers. No bloodsucking agents or business managers. Just get up there and sing, and then pass
around a hat. People pay what they want." Her eyes lit up.
"You could be my guitar player!"

"That'd be great," Armpit agreed. "Except I don't know
how to play the guitar."

Kaira laughed. She tore off a piece of the pastry, dipped
it in her coffee, and tasted it. "Oh, that is so good!" She
dunked a second piece and fed it to Armpit.

The pastry was good, but her fingertips were even better.

"So, how's Ginny?"

"The same," he said. "Great."

"You're so good with her," Kaira said. "I really admire
that. I have a hard time around handicapped kids."

Armpit rarely thought of Ginny as handicapped.

"Have you ever heard of the Make-A-Wish Founda-
tion?" she asked him.

"Yeah, I think so."

"In a couple of weeks I'm supposed to spend the day with
a nine-year-old girl dying of some disease. I was her wish!"

"That's really nice of you."

228

He took a sip of coffee, then wiped the whipped cream off his nose with his napkin.

"I dread it," said Kaira. "I know, that makes me sound like an awful person, but I just get creeped out being around someone like that. My manager says it's good publicity. I don't know what she wants from me! I'm just a singer. It's not like I can cure cancer!"

"She's not expecting you to cure her," said Armpit. "Just look her in the eye. Let her know she's real."

Kaira looked deep into Armpit's eyes.

"Just like that," he said.

She smiled and said, "You are so wonderful."

"No, I'm not," he said.

"Yeah, you really are," said Kaira.

He reached across the small table and held her hand. "There's something I got to tell you," he said.

"Oh, my gosh," Kaira said playfully. "You look so serious."

"It's just that . . ." He wasn't sure how to begin. "You know at the concert, how Ginny and I had counterfeit tickets?"

A man wearing a shirt and tie and one pearl earring suddenly approached the table. "You're Kaira DeLeon, aren't you?"

Kaira took a second, then admitted it. "This is my friend Theodore."

The guy didn't even glance at Armpit. "My niece plays your CD all the time. *The Fountain of Youth,* right?"

"Yep," said Kaira.

"Only one of her CDs I can listen to without throwing up!"

"Uh, thanks, I guess," said Kaira.

"No, really. For overproduced commercial pap, it's not too bad." The guy stretched his arm in front of Armpit's face and said, "I'm very honored to meet you."

Kaira shook his hand.

He handed her a napkin. "Would you mind?"

Kaira showed him her empty hands, but he gave her a pen.

She signed the napkin.

"Thanks. Thanks a lot. My niece will love it. Now will you do one for me?" he asked, handing her another napkin.

"Sorry about that," Kaira said once the guy left.

Armpit shrugged.

"So what were you about to tell me?"

He wasn't sure it was the right time anymore. Everyone in the café seemed to be looking at them.

"About the concert?" Kaira prompted.

Armpit took a breath. "Okay, here's the thing. You know the letter you sent me?"

Kaira laughed. "Yeah, I think I remember it. Talk about embarrassing!"

"Right. So will you write me another letter? One that's not so embarrassing?"

Kaira smiled, then leaned close and whispered, "Maybe it will be more embarrassing."

"No, that's not what I meant. I mean write one some-time this weekend. You don't have to mail it. Just write it in your handwriting and give it to me."

"Why?"

"There's this guy who wants to buy it for a hundred and fifty dollars."

"*What?*"

That came out wrong. He wasn't used to drinking coffee, and it felt like his brain was racing off in different directions.

"Let me explain."

"Yeah, I think you better."

"See, I didn't get the tickets from a scalper. Well, techni-cally I did, but I didn't buy them."

"You're not making any sense."

"See, I have this friend. And he was scalping tickets. We bought twelve tickets for your concert. I paid for the tickets, and he sold them, and we split the profit."

"You're a ticket scalper."

"My friend is. Was. And he's the one who gave me the phony tickets."

"Your friend?"

"But now there's this other guy who will tell the police unless I sell him your letter. So I was thinking if you wrote another letter that wasn't too embarrassing, I could sell him that one, and my friend won't go to jail."

"Why don't I just write you ten letters? Then you can make a thousand dollars!"

"You don't understand. It's not about money."

"No, you don't care about money. Just want to keep *your friend* out of jail."

"Right."

"So how does this *other guy* know about my letter?"

"My friend told him."

"You are unbelievable."

"You don't understand."

"Maybe you should have *your friend* explain it to me!" She stood up. "You're just another hustler. Anything for money."

"What do you know about money?" Armpit asked. "You don't have a clue. You say you want to just sing in places like this and pass around the hat. You wouldn't know how to live like that. Here, buy a jacket. Only a thousand dollars. Charge it to your room. You wouldn't have a clue."

"Oh, I don't have a clue?" asked Kaira. She stood up. "I just have one question," she said. "Who was it who kissed me? You, or *your friend*?"

She picked up her cup and tossed the contents at him, splattering him with coffee and cream.

Several people applauded. A woman in red leather said, "You go, girl!"

She did just that. Right out the door.

Armpit sat there a moment, wiping himself with a napkin as he tried to figure out why Kaira thought X-Ray had kissed her.

32

It was a long walk back to the hotel. Kaira was nowhere to be seen, and he supposed she'd taken a cab. He doubted she had any cash on her, but when she got to the hotel she could probably call somebody to come down and pay the driver.

He headed back up through Chinatown. He wasn't exactly sure of the way, but he knew the general direction. The streets were steeper than he remembered, and after a while he had to take off his coffee-stained sweatshirt and tie it around his waist. He carried Ginny's present in a flat paper bag.

He wondered whether he should try to talk to Kaira when he got back to the hotel, or wait a day, or maybe just fly back to Austin. It would be pretty weird spending the weekend in the hotel with her hating him and everybody on the tour knowing about it. Maybe just write her a note.

He'd thought asking her to write the second letter was such a great plan, but now it just seemed so lame. What good would it have done? Detective Newberg was smart. She'd eventually figure out he was Armpit, whether Felix told her or not.

He had tried to take too big a step, and the current had knocked him off his feet and was washing him away. All his efforts, at school and at work, were for nothing. X-Ray would most likely go to jail, and he probably would too.

For what? The whim of a rich and famous girl.

He had thought he'd made a real connection with her, but what did he know? It wasn't that long ago that he'd thought he made a real connection with Tatiana. The truth was, half the girls at school could have easily won his heart. It wouldn't have taken all that much; just a smile and he'd be hooked.

But would he have thrown his life away for one of them, or was it just because Kaira was rich and famous? He had mocked her for wanting to charge a thousand-dollar jacket to her room, but maybe that was the reason he came to San Francisco, to live that kind of highfalutin life.

No, it was more than that. At least, he thought it was more than that. He didn't know anymore. He didn't know nothing about nothing.

And he had told her she didn't have a clue! *I'm the one who's clueless.*

He took a deep breath. The cool ocean air mixed with the exotic smells of Chinatown. There was something special about being in a strange place, all alone in a mass of people, even if you had just screwed up your life, or perhaps *especially* if you had just screwed up your life.

He stopped and bought some kind of steamed bun, still piping hot, from a Chinese vendor who didn't speak English. The dough was made of rice flour, and it was soft and spongy on the outside. Inside was some of the best roast pork he'd ever eaten.

He was reminded of the speech for Wilbur the Pig. "He'll bring about world peace, and if he doesn't, everyone will get a ham sandwich."

I may have ruined my life, Armpit thought, *but at least I got to eat some really good Chinese food.*

Fred moved with determination along the pedestrian walkway on the Golden Gate Bridge, oblivious to the dirty glances from slow-walking tourists as he elbowed his way past them. His face had the look of pained urgency. He had never lost Kaira before.

Every walker on the bridge, every driver in a car represented danger. Although, really, what worried him the most wasn't some wild-eyed stranger. Sure, Theodore Johnson seemed like a good kid, but what did they know about him? Not much, except that he had a violent criminal history.

Fred made his way past the first tower on the bridge and was able to get a good view of the people up ahead. He spied a person wearing a red sweatshirt, but the person walking next to the red sweatshirt had on a yellow jacket and was too tall.

33

Kaira listened to *Gilligan's Island* in the shower through a special speaker connected to the TV. She would have to leave for the concert in a little over an hour.

Not all the moisture on her face came from the shower nozzle. Some of it came from thinking that nobody would ever like her for who she was, only for what she was.

She'd be glad when the concert started and she could lose herself in the songs. Singing about heartbreak and betrayal would come easy. She'd have to conjure up an imaginary person again for the love songs.

Jerome Paisley knocked on the door to her suite, waited a moment, the slipped a key card into the lock. He opened the door and stuck his large head inside.

"Kaira," he said, but not too loudly. He held the baseball bat. His hands were sweating inside the latex gloves.

He entered and pulled the door gently shut behind him. He could hear the shower running and the sound of the television.

Kaira's suite was bigger than his, with three rooms and a working fireplace. It always bugged him that she got the best room.

The Skipper was yelling at Gilligan.

As Jerome Paisley made his way through the suite, he could feel his blood pounding inside his head. His eyes blurred momentarily, and he stopped to take a breath. So far it had just been a plan, an intellectual exercise by El Genius, but there was a big difference between the planning and the doing.

He gathered his courage and continued into the bedroom. He grabbed hold of a bedpost to steady himself, then waited just outside the bathroom door. The shower was still running.

He heard a rattling noise, then realized that his hand was shaking so much, the bat was knocking against the wall. He hoped Kaira hadn't heard it.

Armpit was winded when returned to the hotel. He had always thought the hills in Austin were steep, but they were nothing compared to where he'd just been. One of the streets was so steep the sidewalk had been shaped to form stairs.

The orange message lights were blinking on his telephones—all five of them. He splashed his face with cold water and watched the phone in the bathroom mirror blink on and off rapidly.

He returned to his bedroom, sat on the edge of the bed, then picked up the phone. He pressed the button for messages.

"*I don't hate you. I'm just sick and tired of being used by everyone. Why should you be any different? Just go ahead and sell the letter. I don't care. I really don't. Everyone else makes money off me, why not you? Besides, how can I be embarrassed? I'm not a real person! I don't have feelings! I'm just a— Just go away. I never want to see you again! You're right. I don't have a clue. But neither do you.*"

Well, he could have told her that.

A new voice came on.

"*That was your final message. To hear the message again, press three. To save it, press six. To erase—*"

Armpit hung up.

Kaira put on a hotel robe. The volume control for the bathroom speaker was to the side of the sink. She turned it down now that it didn't have to compete with the shower.

She towel-dried her hair. Rosemary would come fix it later. She dropped the towel on the floor, opened the bathroom door, and took one step into the bedroom.

Jerome Paisley closed his eyes as he swung.

The bat caromed off her shoulder, then slammed against her throat.

Kaira fell against the bedpost, and before she could even figure out what was happening, she was struck again, this time across her chest.

She found herself on the floor. She tried to crawl under the bed but was only able to partially protect her head. The area under the bed had been blocked off so guests wouldn't lose their keys and underwear.

The bat smashed against the back of her neck just below the base of her skull.

She was only vaguely aware of what was happening as Jerome Paisley grabbed her by the ankle and dragged her away from the safety of the bed. She saw the eerie image of her business manager/stepfather split into two people, each holding a baseball bat high above his head.

There was a noise from out in the sitting area, and then a shout.

It sounded like *the Doofus*!

Jerome turned away from Kaira and swung just as Fred lunged at him. The bat cracked hard against Fred's rib cage, but he kept coming. His hands wrapped around El Genius's thick neck as the two men fell to the ground.

Kaira watched the bat rolled across the floor and under the TV cabinet. She wanted to scream but couldn't get a breath. She tried to crawl to the telephone but couldn't raise herself off the floor.

There was an anguished groan; then Jerome pushed himself up to his knees, took several deep breaths, and stood up the rest of the way. He glanced at Kaira, then went to retrieve the bat.

Fred remained on the floor. Sticking into his stomach was the knife from Armpit's fruit and cheese plate.

The entrance to Kaira's hotel suite had double doors, as it was frequently used to host parties. Armpit was surprised to find one of the doors open. He knocked, and when there was no answer, stepped inside.

He could hear the TV coming from the bedroom. "Kaira?" he called.

Jerome froze. He looked down at Kaira, but she was in no condition to cry out.

"Kaira," Armpit called again.

No answer.

"Look, if you don't want to see me, I understand. I just came to return the letter. I'm not going to sell it. I don't want anything from you."

Jerome moved to the bedroom door, his bat ready. He really didn't want to have to kill Theodore Johnson. That would just complicate things.

Kaira fought to retain consciousness. She tried to call out, but she had nothing left.

Armpit set the letter on the bar. "I'm just putting it right here on the bar," he said.

Good, thought Jerome Paisley. *Touch the bar.*

"Well, I'm going now," Armpit said. "Thanks for the ride. I'll never be the same again."

He waited a moment to see if his little joke might bring her out, but when it didn't, he headed to the door.

Kaira's eyes were closed, but her hand felt around under the night table. Her fingers wrapped around an electrical cord. Using every last bit of strength she had left, she pulled the cord.

The lamp came down with a crash.

Armpit stopped. "You all right?"

There was no answer.

"You okay, Kaira?"

He walked quickly into the dining area, and then on into the bedroom. "Kaira?"

He saw Kaira's stepfather just in time to raise one arm. The bat smashed against it, breaking the bone, and he collapsed to his knees.

El Genius swung again, but Armpit spun away, then pulled himself up with the help of a bedpost.

He saw Fred on the floor, and lots of blood. He didn't see Kaira.

He took several deep breaths as he backed up against the TV cabinet and readied himself for the next attack. His right arm was broken, but he was left-handed.

Kaira's stepfather stepped over Fred as he came at Armpit again, but just as he swung, Fred grabbed an ankle, and the bat smashed into the television set, which exploded in a green flash.

Armpit's left fist was still gaining momentum as it connected just below El Genius's nose, flooring him.

Armpit was all over him, hitting him first with his fist, and then with his elbow on the backswing, again and again, until Jerome Paisley lay motionless.

Kaira's hairdresser, Rosemary, walked into the bedroom and screamed.

34

Amid the chaos of police, doctors, ambulance workers, TV news crew, Kaira's hysterical mother, and other people from the tour all trying to figure out what was happening, Armpit managed to retrieve Kaira's letter from the bar and toss it into the fireplace.

The last he saw of Kaira and Fred, they were being taken out on stretchers. Kaira was unconscious. She had passed out right after pulling over the lamp.

Too dizzy to walk, Kaira's stepfather had to be held up by a couple of police officers as he was led out in handcuffs.

Fred was able to speak just enough to confirm Armpit's innocence, although that really wasn't much of an issue. Armpit would have thought that with him caught in the act of beating up Kaira's stepfather, everyone would have assumed he was the attacker, but nobody doubted his story. Maybe it was his demeanor, or the latex gloves on Jerome Paisley's hands, or the fact that he was the one who had shouted at Rosemary to call the police.

The next twelve hours were a whirling blur of confusion. There was nobody in charge. It was actually Duncan, the bass player, who finally called the Berkeley Auditorium and informed them that there'd be no concert. That wasn't until after eight o'clock.

Twenty thousand people were stamping their feet and shouting, "We want Kaira!" when a man came out and mistakenly announced that Kaira DeLeon had just been murdered. Some people cried, while others were desperately looking for their ticket stubs.

Armpit was questioned four times by the police: first in Kaira's suite, then on the way to the emergency room, where his broken arm was set, then twice more at the police station. He signed a ten-page statement.

He didn't return to the hotel until well after midnight. In the morning he tried to find out if anyone knew anything about Kaira, but nobody did.

The people associated with the tour didn't know what they were supposed to do or where they were supposed to go. Nobody knew who would pay the enormous hotel bill. Aileen, the woman who normally would have been in charge, couldn't be found. She had flown ahead to Portland but never checked into the hotel.

Nancy Young suggested, only somewhat tongue-in-cheek, that Armpit might want to leave now, before he got stuck with the bill. He took a cab to the airport, where he was able to exchange his ticket for the next flight, but there were no first-class seats available. Not that he cared. He slept the whole way home, much to the dismay of the passenger sitting next to him, who kept having to nudge him awake.

"W-were you scared?" asked Ginny.

"It all happened so fast. I just reacted. When I think about it now, I get scared."

"Me too," said Ginny. Her eyes moistened, and she dabbed them with her Golden Gate Bridge scarf.

It felt oddly normal to be back in Austin. "You want to sign my cast?" he asked Ginny.

"Yes."

It was Sunday. They were sitting in his half of the duplex. It was impossible for them to take their usual walk. The street was filled with news vans and camera crews.

Armpit's mother had had to shoo away a number of reporters, local and national.

"He doesn't want to be interviewed!" he'd heard her say. "Why won't you respect his wishes?"

It was nice to hear his mother use the word "respect" when talking about him. But then again, it wasn't every mother's son whose picture was on the front page of nearly every newspaper in the country, usually with the word "hero" somewhere in the headline.

Most of the articles had their facts wrong. According to the Austin paper, Kaira had given him a key to her room, and he had come up for a romantic rendezvous when he discovered she was under attack. An all-news network reported that he was in bed with Kaira when the attack occurred.

What must have happened, he came to realize, was that Fred had left the door to her suite open when he rushed in to save her after returning from his wild-goose chase.

"Does Kaira know you saved her life?" asked Ginny.

"I guess somebody must have told her," Armpit said. "And it's on the news."

"She should call you."

"She will when she gets better. She's in bad shape."

The doorbell rang.

His mother threw up her hands. "Why won't they leave you alone?" She sounded exasperated, but Armpit could tell she loved every minute of it.

"I told you people— Oh." She turned to Armpit and told him a police officer wanted to speak to him.

Detective Debbie Newberg put away her badge as she stepped inside. "Hi, Ginny."

"Hi," said Ginny.

"I need to speak to Theodore alone, if you don't mind."

If Armpit's mother was surprised by any of this, she didn't show it. Armpit figured nothing surprised her anymore.

"C'mon, Ginny, let's see how many people take our picture," Armpit's mother said. She took Ginny by the hand and led her outside.

Detective Newberg joined Armpit on the sofa. "You're quite the hero," she said. Her cheeks flushed pink.

Armpit shrugged.

"I just wanted to let you know I've been assigned to another case. I told my superiors that all my leads had dried up. And really, for just two counterfeit tickets, it isn't worth the resources."

"So you're not going to try to find the ticket scalper?"

Detective Newberg shook her head.

"I see," said Armpit, trying to sound as if the matter was of little importance to him, but a little bit of a smile slipped out despite his efforts. He never had a very good poker face.

"Can I sign your cast?"

"Uh, sure."

He gave her the same marker Ginny had used.

Detective Newberg held his cast as she prepared to write. "So do you want it to Theodore, or to Armpit?"

"Uh . . ."

If this was a test he had just failed it.

She winked at him. "Don't worry. Like I said, case closed."

"So how'd you find out? Did Felix tell you?"

"Felix? He knew?" She seemed genuinely surprised. "No, I just put two and two together and came up with four."

He always knew she would. "I really didn't know the tickets were counterfeit," he said.

"Oh, I figured that, too. The man who bought the real tickets told me that X-Ray had been reluctant to sell them because he'd promised them to a friend. At the time I thought it was just X-Ray trying to jack him around, but then it hit me . . . you were the friend."

"X-Ray's really not a bad guy," said Armpit.

"He'd be all right if he just learned to keep his mouth shut," said Detective Newberg.

He watched her sign her name. "I always liked you," he told her. "I thought you were really cool, and smart, and I really felt bad about lying to you and everything."

Detective Newberg looked up and smiled. "No harm, no foul," she said, then dotted the "i" in her name.

Kaira opened her eyes to see the blurry image of Fred looking down at her. He was wearing a paper-thin blue hospital gown. She might have laughed if it hadn't hurt so much.

"How ya doin?" he asked her.

She tried to talk but could just barely move her mouth. Her face was heavily bandaged. The only nourishment she got was from the IV tube sticking into her arm.

There was something wrong with her vocal cords as well, and she was only able to speak in a kind of raspy whisper. Fred leaned close to hear her.

"Thanks for risking your life for me."

Fred touched her arm. "Just doin' my job, Miss DeLeon."
He winked.

He started to straighten up, but she grabbed his arm.
There was something else she wanted to say. He had to put
his ear close to her mouth to hear her.

"I'm sorry I was such a doofus," said Kaira.

35

Over the next two months, a lot more people signed Armpit's cast, most of them females who decorated their names with hearts and flowers. He didn't get an F in economics, but an Incomplete, which turned into an 89 after he made up the final.

He was very lucky, and he knew it. If Jerome Paisley had succeeded in killing Kaira, Armpit would have spent the rest of his life in jail.

His fingerprints were on the bat. The knife came from his room. Her room key was found in his hotel suite. Traces of his blood and hair would be discovered in the next letter from Billy Boy. Then there was his prior criminal history, and the very public argument at the coffeehouse.

"If I was on the jury, even I would have voted to convict me," he said.

"No, you'da gotten off," X-Ray assured him. "How did you get the bat? You couldn't have brought it from Austin. It wouldn't fit in your backpack. And what? Did Ginny fake a seizure just so you could meet Kaira DeLeon? And you could have gotten Debbie Newberg to investigate for you and she would have found out about the missing money. Besides, how did your hair and blood get inside the envelope? What—did you cut yourself while brushing your hair, while you were writing the letter? The frame was too obvious. If you're going to frame somebody, you got to be more subtle about it."

"You should be a lawyer," said Ginny.

"A lawyer," said X-Ray as he mulled it over. "Now you're talkin'. I'm good at the art of verbal persuasion."

"Otherwise known as BS," said Armpit.

The three of them were sitting in Ginny's room, with all her stuffed animals.

As it turned out, the evidence that would have been used to convict Theodore Johnson would now be used against Jerome Paisley to prove premeditation—to show he had planned to murder her. However, El Genius had pretty much confessed to everything, so it didn't look like there would even be a trial.

Armpit had been a little disappointed when the San Francisco district attorney told him that. If there were a trial then he'd get to go back to San Francisco and see Kaira again. Maybe they would go to Chinatown together and eat a couple of those steamed pork buns.

He still hadn't heard from her. He thought about trying to get in touch with her but didn't know where or how to find her.

"You shouldn't have to call her," said X-Ray. "She should call you! Not even a thank you! She's such an ungrateful—" He stopped because Ginny was there.

"She's going through some hard times," Armpit said.

From everything he'd read in the papers, Kaira's life was a train wreck. That woman Aileen had stolen most of the money from the concert tour, and there were still many people who needed to be paid and ticket holders who needed to be reimbursed. According to the newspapers, Kaira was broke. Whatever money she had left was being eaten up by lawyers and accountants. Of course, he realized, broke for someone like her didn't mean the same as broke for someone like him.

Aileen had been arrested in Belize a few weeks earlier, but the money was never recovered. A police detective had discovered that Theodore Johnson's airline ticket was purchased over the Internet and that the same computer had also purchased a ticket to Costa Rica for someone named Denise Linaria.

Worse for Kaira than the loss of her money was the loss of her voice. The doctors said she might never be able to sing again.

Armpit looked around at Ginny's stuffed animals. Like Hooter, the owl who couldn't see, or Daisy, the dog who couldn't hear, Kaira might be a singer who couldn't sing.

36

But she did sing again.

It was in late February. Armpit was just getting out of bed when he heard her voice on the radio.

> *It's a lost and lonely kind of feeling,*
> *To wake up wearing a disguise.*
> *I lie in bed staring at the ceiling,*
> > *I don't know who I am,*
> > *There's little that I can*
> *Fully recognize. . . .*

Her voice sounded fragile, like fine crystal that might break at any moment, but each note was true and clear. There weren't any backup singers or elaborate instrumentation; just the gentle plinkity-plank of a piano.

> *But I'm taking small steps,*
> *'Cause I don't know where I'm going.*
> *I'm taking small steps*
> *And I don't know what to say.*
> *Small steps,*
> > *Trying to pull myself together,*
> > *And maybe I'll discover*
> *A clue along the way. . . .*

Armpit smiled despite the lump in his throat.

> *Just to make it through the day and not to get*
> > *hurt,*
> *Seems about the best that I can hope.*
> *Like coffee stains splattered on your sweatshirt,*
> > *There isn't any pattern.*
> > *Everything's uncertain.*
> *It's difficult to cope. . . .*

The lump in his throat turned into tears.

> *But I'm taking small steps,*
> *'Cause I don't know where I'm going.*
> *I'm taking small steps,*

And I've forgotten how to play.
Small steps,
> *Trying to pull myself together,*
> *And maybe I'll discover,*
A clue along the way. . . .

The coffee stains were still on his sweatshirt. His mother had tried washing them out, but they were permanently set.

And if someday my small steps bring me near
> *you,*
Please don't rush to tell me all you feel.
You don't have to speak for me to hear you.
> *If I softly sigh,*
> *Look me in the eye*
And let me know I'm real. . . .

Then we'll take small steps,
'Cause we won't know where we're going.
We'll take small steps,
And we'll have too much to say.
Small steps,
> *Hand in hand we'll walk together,*
> *And maybe we'll discover*
A clue along the way. . . .

She didn't say she would see him again, just if. The song could mean anything or nothing at all, he realized. It might just be a song that he inspired, and that was nice too. More than anything, he was just glad to hear her singing again.

Anyway, he couldn't let his life revolve around Kaira DeLeon. He had his own set of small steps to take. 1. Graduate from high school. 2. Attend two years of Austin Community College. 3. Do well enough to transfer to the University of Texas. (Jack Dunlevy wanted him to major in landscape architecture, but Armpit wasn't sure he wanted to dig holes the rest of his life. He was considering studying occupational therapy, so he could help people like Ginny.) 4. Don't do anything stupid. And 5. Lose the name Armpit.

> *Small steps,*
> *'Cause I don't know where I'm goin'.*
> *Small steps,*
> *I just take it day to day.*
> *Small steps,*
> > *Somehow get myself together,*
> > *Then maybe I'll discover*
> *Who I am along the way. . . .*

About the Author

LOUIS SACHAR is the bestselling author of the award-winning novel *Holes*, as well as *Stanley Yelnats' Survival Guide to Camp Green Lake*, *Dogs Don't Tell Jokes*, *The Boy Who Lost His Face*, *There's a Boy in the Girls' Bathroom*, and the Marvin Redpost series, among many others.

LOUIS SACHAR

S M A L L

S T E P S

A READERS GUIDE

1. In the novel, the reader learns about Armpit that "it wasn't really Camp Green Lake that released him from his anger. It was coming home and meeting Ginny" (page 117).What might Armpit and Ginny teach the other characters in the book about taking small steps?

2. Discuss how young people are sometimes driven to make bad choices by the desire—made sharper by peer pressure—for material goods.

3. When Armpit hears Kaira DeLeon sing on the radio at the end of the novel, her song makes him think about his new goals. The last two lines of the song (page 257) are:

    > *Then maybe I'll discover*
    > *Who I am along the way. . . .*

    What do you think is the most important discovery that Armpit has made about himself?

4. There are many situations in the novel in which racism is a factor. Discuss the difference between overt and covert racism as it's depicted in the book.

5. Armpit's parents have an image of the type of people who go to rock concerts. Armpit tells them, "Just because people have tattoos or pierced tongues doesn't mean they're crazy!" (page 94). Discuss the relationships among labeling, image, and prejudices.

6. Armpit takes Ginny to the Kaira DeLeon concert. Why is his mother more worried about Ginny's safety than her own mother is? Discuss why Armpit's mother hesitates when Ginny's mother says, "You must be very proud of Theodore" (page 96).

7. Why does the mayor's telephone call at the end of the novel help Armpit's mother see him differently?

8. Why does Armpit allow himself to become involved in X-Ray's get-rich-quick scheme when he knows he can't trust X-Ray?

9. Armpit believes that the way to turn his life around is to set goals. His five goals are to graduate from high school, get a job, save money, avoid violent situations, and lose the name Armpit. What are the greatest obstacles to Armpit's achieving his goals?

10. On the bus ride from her performance in Baton Rouge to her next show in Houston, Kaira rides with the band members, although she doesn't usually do so (page 67). How is Kaira changed by this bus ride?

11. At the Lonestar Arena in Houston, after the band's one planned encore, why do you think Kaira decides to perform a different kind of song (page 124)?

12. There are many adults in Kaira's life, but she feels she has no one to turn to when she's lonely. Discuss her relationship with one of these adults—her mother, her stepfather/manager, or Fred, her bodyguard.

13. Ginny talks about each of her stuffed animals. What does her commentary reveal about her?

14. Everyone wants friends and listens to his or her friends' opinions. Why do you think Tatiana, who was friends with X-Ray at school, decides at the last minute not to go to the concert with Armpit (page 92)?

15. Armpit and Ginny are unlikely friends. Discuss how people can have preconceived notions about each other and how they can find ways to overcome these ideas.

16. Discuss why you would or would not want to be Armpit's friend.

17. Many of you have read the novel *Holes*, which features the boys in D Tent, among them Stanley Yelnats, Armpit, and X-Ray. At the conclusion of *Holes*, much has changed for the guys who finally get out of Camp Green Lake. The following excerpt about Armpit and X-Ray is from *Stanley Yelnats' Survival Guide to Camp Green Lake*. After you've read (or reread) this scene, and thinking about *Small Steps*, consider how life has changed for Armpit and for X-Ray. In what ways has life surprised these characters, and how has each approached change?

You might say X-Ray survived too well.

From the very beginning, when I was first taken to D tent, it was obvious who was the leader. It wasn't Armpit or Squid, the two toughest guys in the tent. It was X-Ray, a skinny kid who wore thick glasses that were so dirty he needed X-ray vision just to see out of them.

His secret was his confidence and his smile. He was always cool, even in the heat of Green Lake. When he smiled, it made you feel that everything would be all right.

He didn't need to be tough. He had Armpit and Squid by his side. They would do his dirty work for him if necessary, but it was hardly ever necessary. It seemed everyone wanted to stay on X-Ray's good side.

Part of it was survival. I knew that if I was going to survive Camp Green Lake, I couldn't have X-Ray mad at me. But it was more than that. When I did something for him, he would smile his great smile, look me right in the eye, and say, "Thanks, Caveman. You're a good guy." He made me feel cool and confident, too.

He would do things for you—get you an extra piece of bread or a clean pair of socks. Of course, X-Ray never did anything for anybody unless he got something for himself, too. Like the time he saved Zigzag from the B-tent boys and got everyone in D tent an extra carton of orange juice.

The B-tent boys were a couple of years older than us, and they were some of the meanest and toughest guys in camp. One of them was named Thlump, and he was even crazier than Zigzag. I think at one time his name was The Lump, but it turned into one word.

There was a boom box in the Wreck Room. It was a combination radio, cassette player, and CD player, but we were out of range of any radio station, and we didn't have any cassettes. Thlump owned the only CD in camp. It was the first CD put out by the Backstreet Boys. Now, I had always thought only twelve-year-old girls liked the Backstreet Boys, but this was Thlump's lifeline.

Don't get me wrong. I've got nothing against the Backstreet Boys. I'm sure lots of people like their music, but after you've heard the same CD over and over and over again, day after day after day, it becomes a kind of torture. There was one song, "If You Want It to Be Good Girl (Get Yourself a Bad Boy)," which he'd sometimes play five times in a row, while he and his buddies sang along with the chorus.

That was the song that was playing when suddenly Zigzag got up from the floor, walked over to them, and said, "You mind turning that down? I'm trying to watch *Ally McBeal*."

About that time, the chorus kicked in and they

all started singing along. So Ziggy reached over and turned off the music. The entire room became instantly quiet, not just the Backstreet Boys.

Thlump wrapped his big hand over Zigzag's face and pressed his head against the wall. "You're dead," he whispered.

X-Ray instantly eased himself between Thlump and two of his goons. "Hey, guys," he said calmly.

"Stay away, X-Ray," Thlump warned. "I don't want to hurt you, too."

X-Ray showed no sign of fear. "How would you like some new tunes?" he asked.

Thlump still held Zigzag. "You're loonier than your friend," he said.

"What kinda new tunes?" asked one of the goons.

"What do you want?" X-Ray asked.

Thlump let go of Zigzag. "How you gonna get new tunes way out here?"

"I got connections," said X-Ray. "But it's going to cost you."

"It's going to cost *me*?" asked Thlump. "You're lucky I don't kill you and your friend."

"A week's worth of orange juice," X-Ray said. "From you and everyone in B tent."

The B-tenters looked at each other, then back at X-Ray.

"Can you get the Backstreet Boys' second CD?" Thlump asked.

Everyone in the Wreck Room groaned.

X-Ray smiled.

I didn't know how he did it, but two days later X-Ray brought them their CD, and for the next three days, we all got an extra carton of orange juice. It was supposed to be for a week, but after three days, X-Ray told the B-tenters they didn't have to pay anymore. I was disappointed, but who was I to complain? At least I got extra orange juice for a few days, and got to hear some new music, sort of.

Of course we didn't get the extra orange juice for nothing. We each had to give X-Ray half a piece of bread, but it was still a great deal for us.

I saw X-Ray last week. He lives in Lubbock. "He's in his room doing his homework," his mother told me, then pointed the way. "And remind him I'm still waiting for him to take out the garbage."

X-Ray's door was open. I could see him at his desk, which was covered with books and paper. He mumbled something about Angle C.

"X-Ray," I said.

He turned. "Caveman! Good to see you."

His face looked different. It wasn't just that his glasses were clean. He seemed hassled and worn out. Despite the air-conditioning, beads of sweat had collected on his forehead.

I told him I was writing a survival guide to Camp Green Lake and then asked him how he managed to get the new CD for the B-Tent Boys.

He smiled, and for a second he looked like his old self again. "I went to Pendanski," he said. "Asked him what kind of music he liked."

"The Backstreet Boys?" I asked.

X-Ray laughed. "Nah, he'd never heard of them. It was someone ancient and boring. The Rolling Rocks, I think. But I told him they were my favorite group, too. He started naming songs I'd never heard of, and I'd say stuff like 'Rock on' and 'Awesome licks.' Made him feel like he was the coolest cat in the state of Texas."

I could imagine.

X-Ray's mother shouted to him from another room. "Rex, you still haven't taken out the garbage!"

"I got a friend here!" X-Ray shouted back, then continued his story. "So anyway, I told Pendanski, for the sake of camp morale, we should get some new music for the Wreck Room. Except I made him feel like it was his idea."

X-Ray's mother opened the door. She was skinny and wore glasses, too. "I'm not going to tell you again," she said. "And you know the rules about having friends over on a school night."

"He's writing a book about Camp Green Lake," said X-Ray. " I'm going to be in it."

His mother scowled at me. "I'm sorry, but I really

don't want Rex associating with . . ." She paused, unsure of how to put it, but I got the idea.

She turned to X-Ray. "Have you finished your homework?"

"I'll do it!"

"Don't snap at me," his mother warned, then walked out.

He quickly finished his story. Mr. Pendanski was good at computers, so they had no trouble downloading the music off the Internet and burning it on a CD. X-Ray convinced him that the other guys wouldn't appreciate the Rolling Rocks, so they chose the Backstreet Boys instead.

X-Ray looked back down at his homework. "Man, who cares what angles are congruent?"

I shrugged.

"We were supposed to get orange juice for a week," I said. "How come you let them off the hook after just three days?"

"They woulda quit paying anyway," X-Ray said. "This way they thought I was doing them a favor." He laughed. "They owed me."

It was good to see his cool, confident smile again.

"Man, those were the good old days," he said. Then he shook his head and sighed. "Sorry, you got to go. Homework."

On my way outside, I took out the garbage for him.

Some questions prepared by Pat Scales, children's literature consultant

IN HIS OWN WORDS

A CONVERSATION WITH
LOUIS SACHAR

Q: How do you approach your writing?

A: I sit in my office, which is located over the garage of my house in Austin, Texas. My dogs, Lucky and Tippy, are with me. They are the only people allowed in my office when I'm writing. Lucky seems to understand that. He growls at my wife or my daughter if they try to enter. Maybe he senses me growling on the inside. I don't like being interrupted. Writing is a kind of self-hypnosis. Interruptions break the spell, and it's sometimes hard to get back.

Q: You used to be a teacher, as well as a lawyer, but now you write full-time. How often do you write?

A: I generally write about two hours a day, the first thing in the morning. After two hours, I find myself losing energy and concentration. It's best to quit while I'm still excited about the story. Then it will be easier to get started tomorrow. I couldn't write for a longer period, even if I wanted. Tippy has learned my schedule. After two hours, she taps me with her paw, barks, howls, and otherwise lets me know it's time for her walk.

Q: Do you discuss what you've written each day, or wait until the manuscript is complete before sharing it with someone? Can you tell us how you write?

A: I never talk about a book until it is finished. It took me a year and a half to write *Holes,* and I never told anyone anything about it during all that time. I do this for a variety of reasons, but mainly motivation. By not allowing myself to talk about it, the only way I can let it out is to finish writing it. I write five or six drafts of each book. I start with a small idea, and it grows as I write. My ideas come to me while I'm writing. The story changes greatly during the first few drafts. By the time a book is finished, it is impossible for me to say how I got the various ideas.

Q: You dislike hot Texas summers. Since you have not always lived in Texas, please tell us about where you have lived.

A: I was born March 20, 1954, in East Meadow, New York. My father worked on the seventy-eighth floor of the Empire State Building. When I was nine, we moved to Tustin, California. I went to college at the University of California, Berkeley. During my last year there, I helped out at an elementary school—Hillside School. It was my experience there that led to my first book, *Sideways Stories from Wayside School*, which I wrote in 1976. I attended Hastings College of the Law in San Francisco and graduated in 1980. I worked part-time as a lawyer for eight years as I continued to write children's books.

Q: One of your characters, Stanley Yelnats, dug holes in his free time. What do you like to do in your spare time?

A: I like to play bridge and tennis. I'm a much better bridge player than tennis player. Recently, I played tennis with a teacher. She clobbered me. When I found out she was a fourth-grade teacher, I told her who I was. She was very impressed. She couldn't wait to tell her class that she had killed Louis Sachar playing tennis!

Q: Tell us about your family.

A: My wife's name is Carla. When I first met her, she was a counselor at an elementary school. She was the inspiration behind the counselor in *There's a Boy in the Girls' Bathroom*. We were married in 1985. Our daughter, Sherre, was born in 1987.

Q: What are you working on now?

A: I never discuss this, but rest assured, I am always thinking about what will come next. I have many more books to write.

Walking Naked • **Alyssa Brugman** • 978-0-440-23832-4

Megan doesn't know a thing about Perdita, since she would never dream of talking to her. Only when the two girls are thrown together in detention does Megan begin to see Perdita as more than the school outcast. Slowly, Megan finds herself drawn into a challenging almost-friendship.

Code Orange • **Caroline B. Cooney** • 978-0-385-73260-4

Mitty Blake loves New York City, and even after 9/11, he's always felt safe. Mitty doesn't worry about terrorists or blackouts or grades or anything, which is why he's late getting started on his Advanced Bio report. He considers it good luck when he finds some old medical books in his family's weekend house. But when he discovers an envelope with two scabs in one of the books, his report is no longer about the grade–it's about life and death.

When Zachary Beaver Came to Town
Kimberly Willis Holt • 978-0-440-23841-6

Toby's small, sleepy Texas town is about to get a jolt with the arrival of Zachary Beaver, billed as the fattest boy in the world. Toby is in for a summer unlike any other—a summer sure to change his life.

Crushed • **Laura and Tom McNeal** • 978-0-375-83121-8

Audrey Reed and her two best friends are a nerdy little trio, so everyone is shocked when the handsome, mysterious Wickham Hill asks her out. Soon Audrey is so smitten that she hardly pays attention to the vicious underground school newspaper, which threatens to crush teachers and students—and expose some dangerous secrets.

Harmony • **Rita Murphy** • 978-0-440-22923-0

Power is coursing through Harmony—the power to affect the universe with her energy. This is a frightening gift for a girl who has always hated being different, and Harmony must decide whether to hide her abilities or embrace the consequences—good and bad—of her full strength.

Holes • **Louis Sachar** • 978-0-440-22859-2

Stanley has been unjustly sent to a boys' detention center, Camp Green Lake. But there's more than character improvement going on at the camp—the warden is looking for something.

Eyes of the Emperor • **Graham Salisbury** • 978-0-440-22956-8

Eddy Okana lies about his age and joins the army in his hometown, Honolulu, only weeks before the Japanese bomb Pearl Harbor. Suddenly, Americans see him as the enemy. Even the U.S. Army doubts the loyalty of Japanese American enlisted men.

Then Eddy and a small band of Japanese American soldiers are sent on a secret mission to a small island. They are given a special job, one that only they can do.